THE WEIGHT OF WITNESS

UNBURDENED SERIES
BOOK TWO

J.R. GRAY-HEIM

JOSADAH PUBLISHING CO

The Weight of Witness

Published by **Josadah Publishing Co.**

Raeford, North Carolina

Paperback ISBN: 978-1-7373626-7-8

Hardcover ISBN: 978-1-7373626-5-4

Ebook ISBN: 978-1-7373626-6-1

BEFORE YOU BEGIN

FROM THE AUTHOR

While this story may echo parts of our own journeys, I want to remind you—

your story cannot be confined to the covers of a book.

The pages here may close, but your chapters are still being written, every single day.

The Unburdened Series was born from a deep place of reflection—of faith and fear, of belonging and breaking free. For so many within the LGBTQIA+ community, our stories are threaded with both beauty and ache. They hold the weight of silence, of discovery, of learning to love ourselves in a world that sometimes asks us not to.

If these pages resonated with you—if they stirred something heavy, familiar, or even healing—please know this:

You are not alone.

The path to acceptance, to peace, and to joy is ongoing, and you are worthy of every word yet to be written.

When our stories meet trauma, heartbreak, or isolation, they don't end there.

They evolve.

They bloom through resilience, through love, through chosen family and community.

Below are a few places that exist to listen, to help, and to remind you that your story still matters—

and it always will.

Wherever you are, however your story unfolds—

you are seen.

You are valued.

You are loved.

Thank you for walking through these pages with me.

I am deeply honored to share this journey with you.

—**JR Gray-Heim**

<u>LGBTQIA+ Support & Crisis Resources</u>

The Trevor Project — 24/7 crisis and chat support for
LGBTQIA+ youth
thetrevorproject.org
1-866-488-7386 | Text **START** to 678-678

Trans Lifeline — Peer support and resources by and for trans
people
translifeline.org
1-877-565-8860

GLAAD — Advocacy, awareness, and visibility for LGBTQIA+
lives
glaad.org

The National Alliance on Mental Illness (NAMI) — Mental
health and identity-based support

nami.org/LGBTQ

PFLAG — For LGBTQIA+ individuals, their families, and allies
pflag.org

Dedication

For Ms. Bobbie—who made room for me in her family and her faith.
You taught me that who we love cannot separate us from the One
who loves us first. My best friend—may these words reach you
somehow. May heaven keep a porch light on for these pages.

PRELUDE

Unburdened Series: Book 2

Prelude

The months after Heritage changed Van in quiet, irreversible ways.

The church still stood on the corner of Fayette Street with its pink pews and manicured hedges, and he still went most Sundays, sitting in the same spot where he once sang hymns beside Jeremiah. But faith no longer felt like a performance to him. It had softened into something personal, something that belonged between him and God alone.

He found God now in small moments — the hum of the hardware store's fluorescent lights, the smell of sawdust and oil clinging to his shirt after a shift, the cool air drifting through his cracked bedroom window late at night. He prayed less out loud these days, more in thought. Sometimes he wasn't sure if he was praying at all or just remembering how it felt to believe.

He still went to youth group, still bowed his head when others did, but it was different now. His faith grew where silence was allowed to linger.

Colby often sat beside him at church, a familiar shape in the corner of his vision. There was comfort in that — their knees brushing, the small, steadying smile they shared when the choir's voices strained to reach a note too high. They never spoke about what they were, not since the ski trip. They didn't need to. What existed between them had settled into something unspoken, a current moving quietly beneath the surface.

Summer pressed close, heavy and slow. The days stretched long, thick with the smell of cut grass and the whine of cicadas. Van had started working part-time at the hardware store off Branson Street. He liked the rhythm of it — the clatter of tools, the faint metallic taste in the air. He'd begun saving for a car, counting his money in folded bills inside a shoebox beneath his bed. He felt older. More certain. Or at least, that's what he told himself.

Then one afternoon, his mother's voice cut through the hum of the house.

"Van! Honey, come to the kitchen — I want to show you something!"

He rolled his eyes, pushing away from his desk. His first day off in two weeks, and already someone needed him.

"Yes, ma'am!"

In the kitchen, sunlight poured through the window, glinting off glossy papers spread across the counter. *Camp Cardinal's Nest* beamed from the front of a brochure, surrounded by pictures of canoes and smiling faces.

His mother beamed. "We've been saving up and finally got the money to send you to camp this summer! Your father talked to the youth leaders — everyone agrees this'll be great for the youth group."

Van stared at the pamphlet, the cheerfulness of it almost offensive.

"My father planned this?"

"Don't you start," she said, wagging a finger playfully. "You're going, honey. That's final. We already sent the deposit."

He tried to protest — to remind her about his job, his savings, his plans — but she met every excuse with that practiced patience only mothers have.

"And guess what," she added, unable to hide her grin. "Colby and Jeremiah are going too."

The sound of Jeremiah's name landed like a pebble in Van's stomach — small, but heavy enough to ripple.

He mumbled something like *great,* forcing a smile, and retreated down the hallway as her laughter trailed behind him.

In his room, the glow of his computer monitor painted his face blue. The machine hummed, the fan whirring like it was breathing for the house itself. The familiar *You've Got Mail* announcement chimed, bright and intrusive.

Van's inbox was a mess — half spam, half half-hearted job replies — but his messenger list lit up with familiar names: Colby. Jeremiah. A handful of others from church.

He clicked on Colby's name first, sending a simple smiley face and a heart — their quiet code for *it's safe to talk.* No response. The blinking cursor stared back like a pulse.

He hesitated before clicking Jeremiah's name. His fingers hovered, uncertain. *Maybe he already knows about camp.*

The message window opened, and a line appeared almost immediately.

SPORTZ4U2NV: Hey man! Wassup?

TREBLEMAKER16: N2M, u?

SPORTZ4U2NV: N2M, just chillin. Have your parents told you the news yet?

TREBLEMAKER16: Yep, just got the bomb dropped on me five minutes ago. Thoughts?

Van let the cursor blink while he searched the camp's

website, scrolling past staged photos — a mountain lake, a giant lodge, kids in matching T-shirts. He didn't see himself anywhere in it.

Another message appeared.

SPORTZ4U2NV: Well, I actually am looking forward to it.

I think it'll be fun. I'm sure we can all room together. Mom says it's like a dorm setting.

Girls on one floor, guys on the other.

Van typed back, half-distracted.

TREBLEMAKER16: Sounds interesting. Just don't know about the hiking.

Says there's a five-mile wilderness trek overnight in the woods.

Jeremiah replied almost instantly.

SPORTZ4U2NV: Well, at least you still have your sleeping bag that fits two people.

Van froze. The words flickered on the screen, each one tightening the air in his chest. He hadn't expected Jeremiah to bring *that* up — not after so long.

He hesitated before typing back.

TREBLEMAKER16: I'll have to find it. It's somewhere around here.

He hoped that would end it. But another message came.

SPORTZ4U2NV: At least Colby gets the pleasure of having that experience. Guess I missed my chance.

The hum of the computer seemed louder now. Van's heart pounded. Before he could even shape a response, Jeremiah sent another line.

SPORTZ4U2NV: That first night at the ski trip, I heard you guys. I know what happened, and I wished it was me. I know it might be too late, but if you ever want to... the woods will be open to us the whole trip.

The words blurred. His throat went dry.

And then — salvation. A new notification.

Colby.

SOCCRALLSTAR: :) <3

TREBLEMAKER16: :) <3 Just got the weirdest message from Jer. He heard us at the ski trip.

SOCCRALLSTAR: Seriously? What did you say?

TREBLEMAKER16: Nothing yet. He's hinting at it again.

SOCCRALLSTAR: Well, he needs to realize that you belong in my arms and no one else's.

Van smiled despite himself, the tension in his chest easing just enough.

SOCCRALLSTAR: You still feel the same way, right?

He typed quickly, his hands trembling slightly.

TREBLEMAKER16: Of course. No one's arms belong around me but yours.

When he finally turned back to Jeremiah's window, the blinking cursor felt heavier than before. He tried to write something kind, something that would draw a boundary without breaking the friendship.

TREBLEMAKER16: Hey, Jer. Don't beat yourself up. We were all just figuring things out. Col and I aren't putting labels on anything, but I'm not seeing anyone else. I'm happy. I don't want to lose our friendship — not over this.

The response came almost instantly.

SPORTZ4U2NV: I get it. But I'll try to change your mind at camp. You'll see.

Then the chat window dimmed. *User has signed off.*

The room went quiet except for the low buzz of the monitor. Jeremiah always had to have the last word.

Van leaned back in his chair, staring at the ceiling. The fan spun lazily overhead, stirring the thick air. For a moment he thought he could still hear Jeremiah's voice — not the words, but the tone, that pull that never seemed to fade.

He shut the computer down and lay back on his bed. His mind refused to rest. Every thought looped back to Jeremiah — the past, the what-ifs, the danger of it all. He couldn't risk what he had with Colby. But some part of him still burned with a question he couldn't silence: *What if he was right? What if something unfinished was waiting for them at camp?*

The thought lingered as the house fell quiet around him. Outside, cicadas droned in the trees, and the night pressed close — heavy with the weight of witness.

"Every beginning tries to rename you. Keep your name."
—

—VAN'S JOURNAL

CHAPTER 1

A CLEAN SLATE

EARLY JUNE — THE LAST DAY OF SOPHOMORE YEAR

The zipper on Van Shelton's book bag looked ready to split, straining against a mess of crumpled notebook paper, half-broken pens, and the debris of a school year finally finished. He snapped the blue combination lock from his locker, tossed it into the jumble, and slammed the metal door shut for the last time as a Sophomore.

The halls buzzed with end-of-year chaos—shouts, slamming doors, paper airplanes still sailing like someone had just discovered flight. Van adjusted the bag on his shoulder, feeling the weight of the year dragging down one last time.

Sophomore year had begun quietly, his head low, eyes fixed on tile floors. After Heritage and the summer at Cardinal's Nest, he hadn't wanted to draw attention again. He'd promised himself to stay small, unnoticed. But somewhere along the way, that changed. He wasn't sure when it happened—maybe between new friends, a few good grades, or the way people stopped whispering when he passed. He didn't exactly belong, but he didn't feel invisible anymore either.

The thought had barely formed before the bottom of his bag gave way with a groan of fabric.

Books, papers, and loose trash rained across the stairwell landing, scattering into the rush of sneakers and sandals. Anatomy notes slid under vending machines; composition books flipped open and were stamped with footprints.

"Dammit," Van muttered, crouching low and gathering what he could while students pointed or kicked his notes aside. His ears burned.

A voice cut through the noise—bright, lilting, unfamiliar.

"Lord, honey! How in the world do you think you'll get all that back in that bag?"

Van didn't look up, too busy clawing papers into a pile. "Just my luck," he said. "Should've thrown it all away weeks ago."

The girl crouched beside him, curls bouncing as she bent. She pulled a few pens from the floor and handed them over with a grin. "Here, love, let me help. I'm Dana."

Van blinked, remembering her vaguely—quiet in English class after Christmas, the new girl with the Northern accent that never quite fit in Carolina hallways.

They crammed what they could salvage back into the ruined bag. Most of it was useless anyway. Van stuffed the scraps under his arm and stood, catching his breath. Dana handed him his lock, leaning against the wall as if she'd been waiting for him all year.

"You know," Van said, eyeing the gray trash can nearby, "there's nothing here worth saving." He walked over and dumped the whole load—the bag, the notes, the scraps—straight in. Relief washed through him. Symbolic, maybe, but real.

"Thank you," he said when he came back. "Guess the universe was telling me to throw it all away."

Dana's grin widened. "Exactly. Clean slate."

The crowd thinned as they made their way downstairs

together, shoulders brushing now and then. On the landing, Van asked, "Sorry, I don't remember your last name."

"Mitchell. Dana Mitchell. Don't worry, love, I came in late this year."

By the time they stepped into the Carolina heat outside, Dana was already chatting about her summer—her dad, the move from New York, the beach she missed, the friends she'd left behind. Her voice carried both frustration and longing, painting pictures of Orchard Beach bonfires and circles of friends as varied as city streets.

Van listened, nodding, trying not to stare.

Then Dana leaned closer, voice dropping to a conspiratorial whisper. "My best friend back home? Levi. You'd like him. He was the best. Always fun, always dancing, never cared if people stared. And honey—he always managed to have the hottest boyfriends. Made me jealous."

Van blinked, caught off guard. No one in this town talked that freely.

Dana grinned, clearly enjoying his surprise. She studied his face for a second, eyes sharp, then softened with a little shrug. "Anyway... life's too short to be boring. That's what Levi used to say."

Van gave a quiet laugh, his pulse still quick from the honesty of her words. Dana kept talking—about beach trips and how southern sweet tea was "basically syrup in a glass"—and he was grateful she didn't press further.

By the time she scribbled her number and AIM handle on a sticky note and waved goodbye from a white Volvo, Van's mother's minivan pulled to the curb.

She didn't even let him buckle his seatbelt before asking, "Honey, where's your book bag?"

"It broke. Papers went everywhere. I just tossed it," Van said quickly, bracing for the lecture.

His mother sighed, half-scolding but mostly resigned. "Well, you'll just have to ask for a new one for your birthday. Aunt Leslie bought that one when you started middle school—she'll want to know what happened."

Then she pulled into Dairy Queen, the old sign flickering against the afternoon sun.

"You didn't think I'd forget, did you?" she said, putting the van in park.

Van smiled for real this time. Their tradition—sundaes on the last day of school. Just him and her.

"I knew you wouldn't forget, Mom. And this time, I'm getting extra sprinkles."

"Oh, you're a big man now, are you?" she teased, smirking as they walked inside. "Almost seventeen, a senior next year, and suddenly you think the world owes you sprinkles."

Van laughed, the weight of the day easing as the door jingled shut behind them. For a moment, in the sticky sweetness of ice cream and syrup, summer stretched ahead—full of possibility, and maybe, just maybe, something more.

CHAPTER 2

PACKING FOR CAMP

JUNE, THE SUMMER BEFORE JUNIOR YEAR

T he kitchen table looked more like a supply depot than a place to eat. Piles of folded shirts stood at attention beside three kinds of soap, an unopened pack of socks, a flashlight, two bottles of bug spray, and a small mountain of first-aid supplies. The smell of detergent and lemon cleaner mixed with the warm air drifting through the window, heavy with the scent of honeysuckle from the fence line outside.

"Mom," Van groaned from the couch, his arms crossed tight across his chest. "I promise you, I won't need a first-aid kit and instant ice packs. It's camp. They'll have that stuff. I don't want to haul it around on a five-mile hike."

Millie Shelton didn't even glance up. Pencil tapping against her cheek, she read from a yellow notepad like a general giving orders. "You'll need new underwear. A soap holder. Extra tooth-paste, in case you lose yours. And sunscreen — SPF thirty, minimum."

Van stared blankly at the ceiling fan spinning above him. "I never said I wanted to go. I was told I had to."

Millie straightened, her expression caught somewhere

5

between concern and unshakable resolve. "You said you were interested when we first mentioned it."

He sat up, his voice rising. "You and Dad had your minds made up before I even heard about it. You sent the money before you asked me." He grabbed the throw pillow beside him, twisting it in his hands. "And now Emmalee's going too, which means I get to be babysitter for seven days."

His mother's smile didn't slip, but her voice softened. "Van, Emmalee will be in a different part of camp, with her own counselor and her own friends. All you have to do is make sure she doesn't get homesick and that she shows up to meals and services." She said it like a small favor, not a responsibility being dropped squarely in his lap.

He huffed out a laugh that wasn't really one. "Fine. I'll take whatever you want, just please don't buy Lever 2000. It stinks. Get me body wash."

That earned him a side-eye glare, but he was already halfway down the hall. The slam of his bedroom door punctuated the end of the conversation.

LATER THAT NIGHT, the glow of the computer screen painted the walls in cool blue. His AIM window blinked alive, each notification ping echoing through the still house.

SOCCRALLSTAR:

Van, I promise you it'll be great. Tonight at teen church they're picking roommates. Most of the rooms only fit two campers and a counselor. Want to room with me?

Van's pulse kicked. He read the message twice, then a third time. Rooming with Colby. Just the two of them — and a counselor, sure — but the thought still sent warmth up the back of his neck.

He caught his reflection in the dark corner of the monitor,

the faint outline of his face where the screen dimmed. He whispered words he could never imagine saying out loud. *Yes, I'll be your boyfriend. Yes, Colby's my boyfriend.*

By the time he started typing a reply, Colby had logged off. The empty chat box blinked like a heartbeat, a small icon pulsing with a single message left behind: a heart and a smiley face.

The moment hung in the room like the afterglow of lightning.

Then another window popped open.

SPORTZ4U2NV:

HEY BUD! You getting excited yet?

Van's stomach dropped. He hadn't seen Jeremiah at church that morning — hadn't wanted to. Lately, he'd been slipping out early, finding excuses to skip choir, to avoid that voice that still found its way under his skin.

TREBLEMAKER16:

Well, I didn't want to go, but my parents made the decision for me. Could be worse, I guess.

SPORTZ4U2NV:

Man, it's gonna be awesome. Col, Seth, Brandon—we're all going. We'll run the boys' floor for sure.

The words twisted in Van's gut. *Colby and Jeremiah.* Both pulling at him in different ways — one steady and safe, the other a ghost he couldn't quite banish. He stared at the screen until the light blurred his eyes, then closed the window without replying.

He pressed his palms to his face, elbows on his knees, trying to steady the mix of dread and anticipation tightening in his chest. The soft hum of the computer filled the silence — steady, relentless, the same pitch as the noise in his head.

Outside, a train passed somewhere beyond the trees. Its low horn rolled through the night like a warning.

. . .

By Sunday morning, the bags were packed — three of them, bulging at the seams. Van dragged them toward the front door, the new book bag straining against his shoulders. The air already held that damp, Carolina heat that made even mornings feel like mid-afternoon.

"Boy," his father called from the doorway, keys jingling as he leaned against the frame. "Looks like you're moving out for good."

Van didn't answer.

Millie fussed over the luggage, unzipping and re-zipping compartments, her pencil tucked behind her ear like she couldn't stop making lists even now. "Did you pack ties? They might need you dressed up for something."

"Mom," Van sighed, tugging the zipper away from her hands, "Coach Thomas said it's relaxed. No Baptist nooses around our necks."

She didn't laugh. She just smoothed a wrinkle in his shirt and looked at him as if memorizing every inch.

The ride to the church was quiet except for the soft static of the radio. His father cracked jokes about the "peace and quiet" they'd have with both kids gone. His mother sniffled quietly in the back seat, rearranging Van and Emmalee's bags like the right order might make her worry less.

When they pulled into the parking lot, church vans lined the pavement — white with the Heritage logo painted on the sides, their doors open wide. The smell of diesel exhaust mingled with the sugary scent of donuts someone had brought for the trip.

Millie stepped out first and spun Van around by the shoulders, her eyes glistening. "I just worry, honey. You've never been away longer than a weekend."

Van tried to smile. "Mom, it's a week. I'll be fine."

She nodded, but her hands lingered, smoothing the fabric on his shoulders like she could iron away her fear.

Behind them, his father's voice came loud and brittle. "Go on now. Learn how to be a better son and a better man. It's church camp—ought to set you straight."

The words hit the air heavy, sharp enough to sting.

Van swallowed hard, turning toward the vans. Other teens called out across the lot — laughter, shouts, the clatter of luggage rolling over asphalt. The chatter of summer energy covered the tightness in his chest.

He hoisted the bag higher, the strap cutting into his shoulder. Emmalee waved from her spot in line, her ponytail bouncing with excitement.

Van gave a faint smile back before looking toward the horizon — past the steeple, past the rows of cars shimmering in the heat. Camp Cardinal's Nest waited somewhere beyond all that, tucked into mountains and pine trees and a week's worth of sermons and self-control.

Whatever waited for him there — the long hikes, the nights by the fire, Colby's grin, Jeremiah's unspoken words — it would all demand something from him.

Faith. Patience. Maybe even forgiveness.

Van squared his shoulders and stepped forward.

There was no way out now.

CHAPTER 3

AFTER THE AMEN

The powder-blue bus squatted in the church lot like a retired workhorse, its flaking paint chalking the fingers of anyone who touched it. Inside, the vinyl seats clung to bare skin, and the air carried a tired blend of dust, old gum, sunscreen, and the faint tang of Lysol that never quite won its fight. Ceiling fans whirred without helping much. Someone had propped a hymnbook in a cracked window to trap a sliver of breeze.

Forty teenagers poured down the aisle in waves—backpacks thumping elbows, duffels scraping knees—while chaperones called reminders about seatbelts, journals, and "keeping hands to yourselves." Paper rustled. Laughter ricocheted off metal. A harmonica squeaked once, mercifully swallowed by the noise.

"The Guys" commandeered a cluster near the back like they'd paid rent on it. Seth slid in beside Colby, both of them talking fast, their knees bouncing in a rhythm that belonged to private jokes. That left the open space beside Jeremiah.

Van lifted his overstuffed book bag to the rack and dropped into the window seat. The glass breathed heat onto his temple, its edges fogged with fingerprints from a hundred earlier trips. He set his jaw, spine straight, hands flat on his knees.

Jeremiah slipped in next to him, shoulder to shoulder. "Guess we're travel buddies," he said, voice easy, a summer drawl that made everything sound like a dare.

"Yeah," Van muttered, sharper than he meant. "Since no one else wanted the honor."

The words landed brittle. Van felt the sting at once and elbowed him lightly, forcing a laugh soft as paper. "Kidding. Wouldn't sit anywhere else. You always bring the best snacks."

Jeremiah's grin returned. He reached beneath the seat and hauled up a crumpled blue grocery bag. "Told you. Mom loaded me up. Pretty sure she even thought of you." He tossed two Reese's cups into Van's lap, the orange wrappers bright against denim.

Van blinked. "You didn't—"

"She did," Jeremiah cut in, pleased with himself. "Said you're the only one who eats them like they're actual food."

Van fumbled the candies, throat tight. He lifted his chin toward the seat ahead. "Colby! You like Reese's, right?"

Colby turned, his face framed by a cracked green headrest. The smile he threw back could've lit a gym. "You know I can't stand peanut butter. Sticks like paste." He wagged a Starburst packet, then dropped out of sight again, laughter folding into Seth's.

Van's fingers tightened around the Reese's. The bus jolted as last stragglers scooted past, their steps thudding the floor in uneven beats. A chaperone counted heads. Another clapped twice for quiet.

Then polished black shoes clocked onto the first step. Youth Pastor Lane climbed aboard like he was mounting a pulpit— khakis pressed into knife pleats, polo tucked so crisp it looked lacquered. Conversation thinned to a hush not born of reverence so much as routine.

"All right, kids!" His voice carried down the aisle, too big for the metal box that held it. "Eyes up here."

Heads turned. Even the back row halfway straightened.

"You are about to embark on a week of *fun*," he said, drawing out the word until it gleamed, "but more importantly, a week of growing closer to God. Remember: you represent Heritage Baptist in everything you do."

The sentence hung like a sign nailed over the door. Not invitation—warning.

Van's gaze slid to the window. The steeple's white spire cut the blue, shrinking as parents pulled away. Somewhere a dragonfly skittered against the glass, metallic wings catching light.

Pastor Lane kept on, cadence smooth as a Sunday. "You'll make new friends, and you may grow closer to the friends you already have—"

Jeremiah tapped Van's leg twice and whispered below the rhythm of the speech, "Hear that? Even Paster Lane says so. You never know."

"Jeremiah."

The name cracked like a whip. Every eye in the bus snapped to the back row. Jeremiah froze, color climbing his cheekbones, then sat taller.

"Yes, sir," he managed.

Pastor Lane gaze lingered long enough to scald, then moved on. "As I was saying—your behavior reflects on all of us. There will be other church groups at Camp Cardinal's Nest. Not all of those young people will be the best examples. It's your job to know whom to spend time with—and whom to avoid."

Know whom to avoid. The burr of it snagged Van's chest. He could hear the unspoken part as clearly as the spoken.

"Let's pray," Pastor Lane concluded, with the certainty of a benediction already decided.

Heads bowed like wheat in a wind. Hands folded. The driver even dipped for a beat too long before remembering he was meant to watch the road.

Van didn't move.

He watched the parking lot slide past, watched a mother fix her daughter's ponytail in a mirror, watched a father lift a cooler into a trunk and thump the lid twice like sealing a promise. Beyond the curb, heat shivered the horizon. Out there, windows were down and radios were up and no one checked who was looking.

"Dear Heavenly Father…" The words unspooled, low and polished. "Keep these young people safe; keep their eyes fixed on You…"

Van's jaw ached where he held it. These prayers stitched his life together—the same thread looped week after week—and yet somehow they always skipped his name.

"…let their testimonies shine bright; let them bring no shame upon their families, their church, or Your holy name…"

That one slid in like a needle. *No shame.* His father's joke at the curb wasn't a joke at all. His mother's lists. His own carefulness. The right kind of family. The right kind of boy.

"Amen."

The word rolled through the bus like a small wave, lifting and setting everything back in motion. Seatbelts clicked. Wrappers tore. Someone in the middle found a camp song chorus everybody half-remembered. Chaperones compared clipboards.

The powder-blue bus lurched forward, then steadied, humming onto the highway with a rattle that became background if you let it.

Beside Van, Jeremiah tugged a hoodie from his bag and

bunched it in his lap. With a casual flick—too practiced to be innocent—he spread it across both their thighs like a blanket.

Van blinked. "What are you—"

"Relax," Jeremiah said, voice pitched for mischief, a grin tugging one corner of his mouth. "Long ride. Might as well get comfortable."

The cotton held a clean scent—detergent, a trace of cologne. Beneath it, Jeremiah's hand found Van's knee, warm and steady. The gentle squeeze might've passed for friendly if not for the way his thumb rested and didn't move.

Heat jumped through Van like a startled spark. He caught Jeremiah's wrist under the fabric, his own voice thin. "Jere. Not here."

Jeremiah's grin faltered, then returned, smaller. "Just—being close," he murmured. "It's fine."

Van lifted the hoodie edge and slid it off his lap, the fabric puddling between their shoes. He turned toward the window until his forehead met warm glass.

His knee still remembered the pressure. Not like Colby's easy hand at church when a joke shook the pew between hymns. Not like that at all.

Jeremiah leaned back, jitter returning to his leg. The silence between them swelled until the engine's groan seemed to pour into it.

"Hey—what're y'all doin' back there?" Colby's voice cut through, bright as a porch light. He hooked an arm over the seat in front of them and popped up like a magician—one hand gripping vinyl, the other stealing a mini Snickers out of Jeremiah's open bag. He tossed it, caught it, bit it in half.

"We're gonna have a ton of fun this week," he said, eyes skimming Jeremiah, then landing on Van. "Might even meet some new friends."

He winked—easy, nothing on it—and dropped back down

beside Seth, their shoulders knocking, their laughter folding into the engine's drone.

It wasn't much, but the look lingered. Every few minutes, Colby tilted his head just enough to peek back. Each time his gaze found Van—quick, sure—as if counting him present. Still there. Still okay.

Jeremiah noticed. The chatter sharpened at his edges; his leg bounced faster. If Colby was going to watch, Jeremiah was going to *occupy*.

The bus ate miles. Pine gave way to pasture, then returned thicker, taller, as the foothills shouldered into view. Billboards hawked fireworks, boiled peanuts, Jesus. A hawk wheeled a lazy circle over a field cut to stubble. Cicadas shrieked in waves that rose and fell as if the forest breathed.

A chaperone walked the aisle, hand on each seatback for balance, checking off names against a list already heavily notated. "Devos at nine. Lights out at ten. Hiking groups sorted when we arrive. If you have *medical needs*"—her eyes flicked to Van's row and the candy spread there—"you should've packed accordingly."

Seth started a monosyllabic chant to a drumbeat tapped on the seat frame. Someone answered with a kazoo line that earned a threat to confiscate all instruments of *noise and Satan*. Laughter broke; the rhythm continued softer.

Van laid his temple to the window and let the landscape smear to watercolor. In the glass he caught his own outline—mouth a firm line, eyes tired in the kind of way sleep didn't fix. He counted exits like prayer beads.

"Want the Reese's?" Jeremiah asked at last, small. "I... grabbed them for you."

Van looked down at the orange wrappers still in his lap. He would eat them later, alone, when the sweetness wouldn't confuse gratitude with anything else. "Thanks," he said. "I'll save them."

Jeremiah nodded, mouth pressed into a line that meant he'd heard more than the words.

The powder-blue bus climbed, engine complaining as the grade steepened. The air lifted cooler. A strip of lake flashed through the trees—blue as enamel—then vanished. The road curved. The sun glanced off a distant cross on a hill and struck the aisle like a thrown coin, bright, quick, gone.

Pastor Lane stood again as if the aisle were his, passing a hand lightly over headrests, addressing each pocket of teens with that practiced warmth. "Remember, we travel as a testimony," he said, and teens nodded because nodding was what you did.

Van kept his eyes on the ribbon of highway unwinding ahead, a line drawn toward something decided before he boarded. Whatever waited—devotions, hikes, the fire's smoke in his hair, Colby's winks, Jeremiah's restlessness—would arrive in its own order.

He flexed his fingers once against the cool glass and made himself breathe slow, like he did between songs when the sanctuary still held the last note.

If God is anywhere, he thought, watching sunlight break and scatter on the bus's crooked windshield, *He can handle the space between who they want and who I am.*

The bus dipped into shade. Ahead, the mountains rose like a promise they might or might not keep.

CHAPTER 4

ARRIVAL AT CAMP CARDINAL'S NEST

SUNDAY AFTERNOON — ARRIVAL DAY

The bus shuddered into the gravel lot and gave a last, exhausted sigh. Brakes squealed like a hymn sung off-key, and a veil of dust lifted, turned to gold in the sunlight, and settled over everything—the vans, the duffels, the day.

For a breath, no one moved. Then the doors hissed, and the valley's breath rushed in—pine-sweet, damp, and hot enough to iron creases out of shirts.

"All right, y'all, let's move it!" a chaperone clapped, as if applause could push forty teenagers through a doorway at once. "Grab your bags. Don't leave anything behind. Counselors are waiting."

The aisle clogged instantly. Suitcases thunked from the racks; duffels scraped shins; pillows were pinned under elbows. Voices stacked on top of one another—groans, jokes, names being tried out loud just to hear how they'd sound this week.

Van stayed seated a beat longer, forehead against the warm window, taking the lay of it. The valley unrolled like a diagram designed by a stern hand.

Dorms first—two squat rectangles of beige-painted

concrete, boys to the left and girls to the right, identical except for the oversized wooden placards bolted above their doors. Cinderblock corridors showed narrow windows propped just wide enough to let thin curtains breathe. Order had been chosen over comfort and then nailed in place.

Beyond them, above all of it, the chapel and the mess hall sat on the ridge like sentries. The steeple's cross caught the sun. The cafeteria roof stretched beside it, low and practical. And stitching steeply between valley and ridge was a staircase cut into the hill—stone, pale, relentless. Each step baked bone-white.

Around Van, the commentary started up.

"Dang, that's a hike."

"Bet we do it three times a day."

"I didn't sign up for boot camp."

Van's stomach sank. The whole layout felt intentional—like someone had traced lines on a map and said, *Make them earn their meals. Make them climb to God.*

"Van, you comin' or what?" Jeremiah stood in the aisle already, duffel slung careless over one shoulder, smile hot enough to burn through dust.

Van rose. The suitcase handle bit his palm. He let the tide of bodies carry him out to the heat, to the crunch of gravel under rubber soles, to the sun that pressed hands flat against his shoulders like a parent about to deliver a lecture.

Chaperones flapped clipboards like fans. "Boys here! Girls over there! Line up, line up!" The teen herd funneled into crooked rows, luggage at their ankles, sweat already scoring salt tracks at hairlines.

Van's eyes returned to the staircase and stayed there. It wasn't just the climb. It was the kind of place that made you look up—whether you wanted to or not.

"Welcome to Camp Cardinal's Nest!" A counselor bounded

forward, ponytail bouncing, her smile trained for distance. "We are so glad you're here to grow in faith this week!"

A cheer rose halfway, fell apart in the heat, and reassembled as scattered claps.

They introduced themselves in turns. Jake—tan, gel-slick hair, shoulders cut by summer—flexed while saying the word *Jesus* and drew squeals from a trio near the front. Mason, tall and grave, spoke like he had somewhere more important to be with his Bible already open on his lap. Emily, neon scrunchie bobbing, pinwheeled energy and exclamation points and made Emmalee across the way wave like she'd found a favorite cousin.

Van heard around them more than through them. The chapel glittered high above, and the staircase insisted on itself the way a rule does.

"You'll be representing your families, your church, and most importantly, Christ this week," Mason said, letting his eyes sweep like a searchlight. "Your words, your actions, even your attitudes matter."

Nods followed as if attached to strings.

Jake clapped his hands. "Let's get you to your dorms and meet your roommates!"

Cheers, groans, the scrape and shuffle of forty bodies relocating as clipboards began calling names into trios—three campers to a counselor, a tidy geometry of oversight.

"Van Shelton. Jeremiah Richardson. Tyler Brooks," a voice rang out, sharp enough to cut through everything.

Van's suitcase lurched as he dragged it forward. Gravel fought his wheels. *Of course* Jeremiah's name paired with his. Of course.

Then he saw the counselor waiting with their card.

Scottie.

Taller than most of the adults, slim lines edged in summer

muscle beneath a crimson camp polo. Sun-burnished forearms freckled copper. Hair long enough to curl at the edges where sweat dampened it against his neck. A smile that made you want to behave.

"This is my cabin group, then?" he asked, tucking his clipboard under one arm. The other hand extended, grip firm and sure. "Jackson Scott Addington the Third. Everybody calls me Scottie. You boys can too."

Jeremiah shook like he'd just met a celebrity. Van hesitated, then took the hand that swallowed his with warmth and no judgment.

"I know this place can look big on day one," Scottie said, thumb resting on the worn spine of the hunter-green Bible tucked beneath his arm. Its leather edges were softened, pages fat with underlines. "I sat in these same rooms with my brothers, climbed that hill more times than I can count. Didn't have all the answers then. Don't have 'em now. But I know where to look." He tipped the Bible, not theatrical, just true.

Van's throat tightened at the plainness of it. No flex, no flourish. Just a person built out of summer and scripture and steadiness.

Jeremiah had already thrown his duffel onto the bottom bunk of the assigned room like planting a flag. Tyler arrived with the thump of a bag and the guarded eyes of a kid who wanted to be left alone. Sandy blond mop, sunburn blooming across his nose, jeans cuffed too high over socks pulled too tall.

"Guess we're stuck together," he said, squatting to unzip and fish out a stack of comic books. "Long as y'all don't snore, we'll get along fine."

"Bottom's mine," Jeremiah announced, swagger lazy and practiced. "You can fight Shelton for the top."

Van didn't. He hauled his suitcase up the squealing ladder and let the thin mattress take the weight he didn't want to show. The room smelled like Pine-Sol and summers layered into cinderblock—the flat tang of cleaner over damp wood, over boy, over years.

Down the hall, a door was propped open by a brick. Van followed the hive-sound of voices and the slapping punctuation of flip-flops and found the bathroom.

A rank of white sinks marched beneath a row of scratched mirrors. Stalls gaped and clattered as boys tested locks. Beyond another doorway, the showers: ten narrow rectangles, five to a side, thin partitions, no curtains. Water would run loud there, voices echoing, steam erasing faces until they were only outlines.

Van's stomach tipped. The thought of standing in that steam with Jeremiah's voice somewhere in it—of eyes landing where he couldn't manage them—sent static up his arms.

He backed away, knuckles whitening on the bunk ladder.

"What's wrong?" Jeremiah sat up, following Van's gaze.

"Nothing," Van lied, rolling onto the top bunk and laying himself flat like a plank. The ceiling had hairline cracks he could map into rivers if he needed to calm down.

Seven days, he counted. *Seven days of sinks and stalls and pretending.*

The dinner bell—really a length of iron hung from a frame—clanged from outside, the sound bouncing off cinderblock and spilling down the hallway.

"Meet-and-greet time, boys!" Scottie leaned into the door, his polo dark at the collar with heat, his grin cut wide. "Up the stairs—let's move!"

The stairs.

By the third switchback, Van's thighs burned. A river of kids climbed in clusters—girls laughing too loud to keep balance, boys shoulder-checking for sport, counselors calling names like shepherds with clipboards. Jeremiah kept just behind Van, close enough that Van could hear him breathing; Tyler trudged alongside, comic books tucked against his ribs like contraband scripture.

The Great Room at the top spread its ribs wide—heavy beams overhead, strings of white lights draped between them, rows of folding chairs set in hopeful perfection. A small stage held a podium, a microphone, and a wooden cross polished to a shine that snagged and threw the light.

"Saved us spots," Scottie called, one hip hiked against an aisle seat to block three in a row near the front.

Van took the one by the aisle. Jeremiah dropped into the middle, pleased with proximity. Tyler slouched on the end, arms crossed, expression settled on *prove it.*

The room filled and softened into a big hum. Counselors worked the rows, clapping shoulders, high-fiving, corralling outliers with practiced warmth. Different kinds emerged if you watched—Jake leaning and collecting giggles; Emily dotting programs with hearts as she handed them out; Mason already moving his lips over a verse like he was lapping the field before the starting gun.

"Okay, campers!" A director's voice hit the mic, bright enough to dent the air. "Let's get to know one another. When I point, stand up, name, home church, and one fun fact!"

Groans rolled the room.

Names tumbled: Megan from Shiloh who loved horses; Ryan from Fellowship who could juggle; a boy who could burp the alphabet; a girl who'd met a Christian recording artist and had the selfie to prove it.

The finger landed on Van.

He rose slow. His knees weren't sure about standing for a room all at once. "Van Shelton," he said, and cleared his throat. "Heritage Baptist. And, uh... I like to draw."

Polite clap. The heat behind his ears pooled into his collar.

Jeremiah leaned in, whispering without moving his mouth, "Should've told 'em you're great at avoiding fun."

Van's lips twitched despite himself.

Seth elbowed the back of a chair and grinned across the aisle. "Shelton's fun fact is hauling everybody's luggage," he stage-whispered. "Standing O, guaranteed."

Laughter hit in a little wave. Even Colby's laugh—warmed by the day, careless—joined it, and for a heartbeat Van hated the way it landed heavy even when it was only a joke.

"Nah," Colby said, turning back, cheeks flushed. "He should've said he wins the award for sleeping through Sunday School." It was light; it still pinched.

"At least I don't snore through sermons," Van shot back, sharper than he'd meant. A chorus of *ooo* rose. Jeremiah's knee found his under the chair—one quick nudge, approval disguised.

Scottie lifted a hand, not scolding—steady. "Keep the jokes kind," he said, smiling through the line. "We're here to build each other up." He didn't raise his voice, but the row settled as if he had.

Games came next—Two Truths and a Lie, Find Someone Who...—designed to mix kids who didn't want mixing. The boys fanned out just far enough to fulfill the assignment, but their orbit stayed tight, pulling them back toward Colby like gravity. Van drifted in the pull, accomplishing the tasks with a pen and a square of paper and a face that could pass for engaged.

He noticed the glances. Scottie's when he was sure no one else needed something. Jeremiah's—restless, scanning, landing on Van a beat too long. Colby's occasional check-back, quick and certain, like counting heads and finding his person still there.

When Scottie shared the closing devotional—a few quiet

verses about mountains and eyes lifted and paths made straight —his voice filled the rafters without trying. Van let the words bank off his ribs and settle where they would. The final "Amen" quivered the folding chairs.

He whispered his own *amen*, smaller, and kept his gaze on Jeremiah. For a half-second, Jeremiah's eyes met his. It felt like the tiny click of a latch.

Night drew itself over camp in layers, moths trading the last of the sunlight for bulbs. Back in the dorm, boys negotiated space with the same clumsy diplomacy they used for jokes— too loud, then too soft, then settled. Metal frames squealed as weight shifted. Towels hung in a line from the single hook on each bedpost like flags surrendering.

The door opened.

Scottie ducked in, camp T-shirt swapped for a softer one, Bible tucked snug under his arm. Without ceremony, he stepped to the bottom bunk nearest the door and dropped his duffel.

"That one's mine," he said, friendly as a posted rule. "Counselors get the bottom by the door."

Tyler's head popped over his comic like a prairie dog. "There's three empty ones," he groused. "Why this one?"

"So I'm first to hear if somebody tries sneakin' out or stumbling in," Scottie said, smiling in a way that left no purchase for argument. He tapped the Bible lightly against his palm. "Keeps y'all out of trouble. Keeps me honest."

Jeremiah snorted. "Translation: he doesn't trust us."

"You catch on quick," Scottie shot back, grin widening.

Tyler slung himself up to the top bunk with a theatrical groan and flopped onto the mattress so hard the springs answered in protest.

Scottie slid his Bible onto the narrow shelf and stretched out, long legs crossed at the ankles, hands laced behind his head. "Lights out means quiet," he said, yawning around the words. "Early morning tomorrow. Breakfast at seven. Chapel at eight. Hiking groups posted after."

"Do we get curtains in the showers?" Tyler asked, not looking up from his comic.

A ripple of laughter eased the air. Scottie lifted a brow. "You'll survive, Brooks."

The overhead bulb hummed, casting a thin wash that made freckles bloom across Scottie's forearms and threw ladder shadows up the wall. Van pulled the thin blanket to his chest. It wasn't just the showers anymore, or the sermons, or the stairs that turned knees to rubber. It was the simple fact of proximity —for seven nights, the steady rise and fall of Scottie's breath at the door like a metronome, the sense that someone decent would hear if he cracked.

He turned onto his side and studied the hairline crack in the ceiling until it became a river system again. In the bunks below, Jeremiah shifted, the mattress springs answering. Tyler sighed and flipped a page. Somewhere down the corridor, a toilet flushed and a boy coughed and the bell's earlier clang remembered itself in the pipes.

Van closed his eyes and breathed slow until the tightness in his chest thinned. Outside, the pines stitched their needles against a sky gone black and jeweled. The hill waited for morning. The chapel waited above it. The week gathered itself, patient.

Close enough to hear. Close enough to notice.

And that, more than the climb, made the days ahead feel long.

CHAPTER 5
FIRST MORNING
MONDAY AT DAWN — CAMP CARDINAL'S NEST

The bell split the valley clean in two.

Metal on metal—three hard strikes—rang off the ridge line and rattled the thin dorm windows in their frames. Van jerked awake into the blue-gray between night and morning, heart hammering, unsure for a breath where he was. Then the room came back: cinderblock walls sweating in the humidity; four bunks; the sour-sweet mix of Pine-Sol, boy, and damp canvas.

Across the aisle, Scottie was already up, stretching like he'd been awake for hours. The floor creaked under his weight as he rolled his shoulders back, freckles bright in the dawn wash.

"Rise and shine, fellas!" His voice filled the small room without trying. "Big day ahead. Don't keep the Lord waiting."

From the lower bunk, Jeremiah dragged a pillow over his face. "It's not even light out."

"Exactly," Scottie said, grinning. "Mercies are new every morning. And morning starts now."

Tyler pushed a comic off his chest and sat up, hair roostered in six directions. "Feels illegal," he muttered, scrubbing his eyes with his fists.

Van swung his legs over the edge. The mattress springs squealed their protest; gravity felt doubled, like the night had draped a lead apron over him. He planted his feet on the cool concrete and waited a beat for his balance to catch up.

Out in the corridor, the herd had already started moving. The bathroom was a bottleneck of humanity: boys shoulder to shoulder at the sinks, toothpaste foam sliding off chins; deodorant fog in the air—cheap, sharp, asserting itself; stall doors clapping shut and bouncing open; shower valves cranked until pipes groaned.

"Come on, Shelton." Jeremiah shouldered him lightly toward a sink. "Don't primp. We got chapel to not sleep through."

Van cupped water to his face—cold enough to sting, clean enough to wake—and kept his eyes on the spidered mirror. He rinsed his mouth, letting the roar from the open showers stay where it was: behind him. Voices bounced off tile; towels snapped; bare feet slapped wet concrete. He stayed at the sink, deliberate, working slow, pretending a hangnail demanded surgery.

"Move it along, gentlemen." A counselor's voice slid down the row.

"Yessir," Van said to the mirror, and stepped sideways without turning his head.

BREAKFAST BARELY TOOK the pressure down. The mess hall buzzed like a hive—trays clacking, plastic utensils skittering, a hundred conversations layered into a warm hum. Windows on the far wall caught a soft ribbon of lake and threw it back in strips across aluminum pans of eggs and biscuits.

"Fuel first." Scottie shepherded their four through the line, one palm easy at the small of Tyler's back when the kid stalled.

He clapped Van's shoulder as he passed a ladle of gravy. "Eat up, Shelton. Hill's not getting shorter."

Van nodded, grip tight on the tray. The eggs were rubber; the gravy tasted like the inside of a paper cup; the biscuit made an honest try at being bread and didn't quite make it. He chewed anyway.

Across the room, Colby sat with Seth and Brandon, telling a story with his hands, laughter rolling from their table in warm waves. Every time Van's gaze snagged there, he made himself look away—back to the beige of his plate, the shine on Scottie's Bible even at breakfast, the list tacked by the serving window: **7:00 Breakfast, 8:00 Chapel, 9:00 Field Rotations.**

Jeremiah dropped his tray across from him, grin already lit. "Day One, baby." He thumped the table with his fist, then stole Tyler's orange, which earned him a half-hearted glare.

"Return the citrus, Richardson," Scottie said mildly, not looking up from folding his hands over his Bible. The orange rolled back across Formica like a small confession.

Van chased his last bite of biscuit with lukewarm milk and tried not to picture the staircase.

THE CHAPEL SAT at the valley's crown, timber-framed and taller inside than it looked from below. Light came in sheets through high windows and laid itself across polished planks. A cross hung at center, naked wood, no adornment, gleaming where a beam of sun found it.

They filled in: row after row, the room taking their weight like it had been built for this moment. The camp band struck a chord that wobbled for a breath and then found itself. Counselors clapped on two and four; kids stood; a microphone coughed; a projector blinked a lyric into being.

Scottie steered their cluster toward the front he'd staked

early. Van slid into the aisle seat. Jeremiah took the other side like wind taking a door. Then Colby—Colby slipped into the space beside Van, shoulders aligning, knee brushing once and staying put like it belonged there.

"Hey," Colby murmured, a small smile already at the corner of his mouth, the word edged in soap and sun.

Van's chest tightened. "Hey." He made a show of flipping the paper program open, as if someone might grade him for it.

"Didn't think we'd end up up front," Colby whispered. "Everybody can see us."

"Guess we'll have to behave, huh?" Van returned, aiming for light and hitting shy.

Colby's smile deepened, then the singing swallowed space for talk. **"Victory in Jesus"** rose high and familiar, the rafters catching the sound and sending it back polished. Arms lifted. Some swayed. Some mouthed. Some belted. The floor thrummed with sneaker taps.

Van let muscle memory carry his lips. His mind kept tacking sideways—to the warm press of Colby's shoulder; to the way Colby's eyes went soft and far when he sang; to the knowledge that Colby was the kind of boy counselors pointed to when they talked about *calling*.

He glanced. Caught. Colby's eyes were open, too. A small private spark crossed the inches between them, a yes without a voice. Van felt the hitch, the pull.

An elbow from the other side broke it—Jeremiah, smirking. "It's just church, Shelton. Smile like you mean it."

The prayer that followed drew heads down like dusk. Van bowed with everyone else, then let his eyes slit a fraction. From here, the room looked like a field in a gentle wind—shoulders rising and falling; mouths shaping words only God was meant to hear. Colby's eyes were not closed. They were tipped toward

Van's hands, and when Van noticed, Colby let his gaze climb to meet his and pause there, steady.

"Amen," the room breathed, and the spell folded up neat as paper.

Colby clapped on tempo, easy. The small smile vanished back into the role he wore so well. But the click of that unseen latch still rested under Van's ribs.

THEY SPILLED from the chapel into full sun, chatter rising like birds when a gate's unlatched. Clipboards waved. "Field—this way! Devotion groups—by the oak! Water stations are along the fence—hydrate!"

The guys gathered under the flagpole like they'd been magneted there. Seth elbowed Brandon and nodded toward a knot of girls in the pine shade. "Yellow top. Tell me she ain't the cutest here."

Brandon cut a look toward a high ponytail. "Nah. Ponytail wins."

Jeremiah rocked back on his heels, hands in pockets. He waited for the beat where attention was primed, then threw the line. "Y'all can fight over 'cutest.' Me? Pastor's son. House odds."

Laughter hit like applause. Knuckles rapped his shoulder. Crown awarded.

Colby chuckled, but when the noise thinned, he shrugged. "I don't know, man. I'm here to grow closer to God this week."

Groans. "You can flirt and grow closer to God," Seth declared. "That's how camp works."

They moved on—ranking, trading, letting their words skim the surface. But *grow closer to God* snagged Van and held.

If closeness to God meant stepping back from whatever this was—late-night drives, shared jokes that felt like secrets, the quick glance in a pew that said more than a paragraph—then where did that leave him? Was he the thing Colby would lay down as an offering?

He shoved the thought to the side, but it sat like a stone in his pocket.

THE BACK FIELD turned into organized chaos. Cones sprouted. Whistles pierced. Counselors split teens into circles and lines that dissolved and reformed like schools of fish.

Seth spun through all of it with endless fuel. Brandon strutted jokes into being. Jeremiah ran a commentary under his breath that made the brunette next to him double over. Colby didn't command the space, but it bent toward him anyway—steadying a kid who tripped, sprinting unasked after a runaway ball, clapping for the wrong team on purpose when somebody needed a little light. The kind of goodness that didn't announce itself and was therefore impossible to ignore.

"Shelton, you're up!" a counselor barked.

Van lurched forward. Baton. Sprint. Breath burned bright in his chest. He slapped the handoff into Seth's palm and staggered to a stop.

"That's it, Shelton!" Seth whooped, clapping his back. "Knew you had it." Just words. They landed like water on a dry throat.

Van looked for Colby—found him laughing with an arm slung across another boy's shoulders, his head tipped back. The stone in Van's pocket got heavier.

"Pick a partner!" someone shouted for the three-legged race.

The boys scattered like coins. Seth vanished toward yellow top; Brandon toward ponytail; Jeremiah toward the brunette. Van stood stupid in the middle of it—ankles tingling with the memory of stepping in time, chest tight with the old fear of being the last unpicked chair when the music stopped.

"Hey." Colby's voice, right at his ear. When Van turned, he was there already, half-smile like an offered hand. "Guess we're stuck together."

Relief came so fast it made Van lightheaded. "Guess so."

They knotted the red bandana around their ankles. The whistle blew. They pitched forward, immediately a tangle— left-right-left—with Colby's palm firm at Van's waist to keep them upright.

"Left, then right!" Colby laughed. "Count it."

They found it—awkward to decent to good—bodies learning the same beat. Counselors yelled. Teams crashed. Grass stained their calves. Each time they stumbled, Colby's grip tightened; each time they sailed, Van felt his pulse rise into his throat.

They crossed mid-pack, breathless and grinning. "Told you we'd figure it out," Colby said, fingers lingering on the knot an unnecessary second before tugging it loose. The look that followed held for a breath longer than a look needed.

"Yeah," Van said, aiming for even, landing on hoarse. "Eventually."

But the words from earlier kept tolling under it all. **Grow closer to God.** Did that mean stepping back from this warmth as easily as they untied the bandana?

BY EVENING, the day had worked its hours through them. Showers (Van's avoidance plan: soap-and-washcloth at the sink while the herd thundered; he'd try for a late-night window when the hall went quiet). Dinner. A sunset that poured itself down the ridge like honey. Fireflies popping the field into constellation.

Scottie gathered their cabin in a circle before lights-out, Bible open across his lap. The lamplight softened his freckles; the day's sun had left the bridge of his nose a little pink.

"This week's about naming what pulls at you," he said. "Not so you can be ashamed of it. So you can put it in the light and see it clearly." His thumb rode the Bible's worn edge. "Distraction's not always evil. It's just anything that keeps you from hearing what God's already saying."

The room quieted in the way of a pond when wind drops.

Jeremiah went first, because of course he did. "My struggle?" He slouched deeper, grin crooked. "Staying focused. A lot of... distractions here." The pause was suggestive on purpose. Laughter loosened the circle.

Tyler grunted something about missing home and how people breathed too loud at night. Scottie nodded like that was sacred truth, too.

Colby's turn. He looked down at his hands. "I just want to make sure I'm walking the right path," he said, voice low. "Not letting anything pull me away from God."

Safe words. Church words. They still found their mark. If *anything* meant *anyone*, then Van knew exactly where he fit in the schema—as a current, a tug, a thing to resist.

When it came to him, Van said, "Staying positive." He pushed air through the sentence. "Not letting my head write stories that aren't true." Scottie's eyes flicked up—interested, not invasive—and he nodded once like they could come back to that thread later and tie it off tight.

They bowed their heads. A prayer like a clean shirt: nothing fancy, well-worn, fit right.

Van's eyes stayed shut until amen. When he cracked them a sliver, Jeremiah's stayed open, gaze steady across the small circle, not at Scottie, not at the floor—at Van. It wasn't a leer. It wasn't a dare. It was a look that said, *I still see you. Even in this light.*

The circle broke. Metal sang under shifting weight. Scottie stood, stacked the chairs two at a time, and set his Bible back on the shelf. "Lights in five, boys," he said, and yawned like a human being instead of a statue.

Van climbed to the top bunk and lay on his side, palm flat on the sheet to quiet its rattle. Down the hall, water in the pipes remembered the day. Outside, the bell that had ripped the morning now hung dark and quiet against its frame.

He stared at the hairline crack and let it become a river again, forked and winding. *Grow closer to God,* he thought, and tried to imagine a version of that where he didn't have to cut himself in half.

Sleep came slow, then all at once, like stepping off a ledge you didn't know you were standing on.

CHAPTER 6

MORNING HEAT

MONDAY — FIRST FULL DAY

T he air in the dorm had already thickened by the time the gray before sunrise laid a thin stripe across the floor. Heat rose from the concrete like breath; the camp sheets clung to damp skin and made a second, unwilling shirt of themselves. Somewhere down the corridor a door squeaked wide, then a whistle chirped twice—thin, bright, impossible to ignore.

Van stared up at the hairline crack in the ceiling until it branched into a river system again. Last night's words kept drifting back across it like leaves. **Grow closer to God.** Colby had said it gently, like a thing you were supposed to say. It still felt like a line drawn in chalk between them—easy to smudge until you looked down and realized you'd crossed it.

The hinges complained. A draft tugged the blinds. Scottie stepped in from the showers with his hair dark and dripping, a towel knotted low and the faint steam of clean water following him like a small weather system. He crossed to his duffel humming the ghost of a hymn, nothing you could sing along to, more like the memory of one.

Van's breath snagged. He told himself to roll over, to make a show of sleep. He didn't. He felt the room narrow around the small, ordinary things: the bright scatter of freckles in the blue wash of morning; the easy economy of movement; the patient Bible on the nightstand waiting to be picked up. When Scottie bent to reach for the camp polo, the towel shifted and the moment almost tipped out of ordinary into something else. Van turned his face to the pillow a beat too late. He inhaled cotton and detergent and counted to five.

By the time he looked back, Scottie was already tugging the polo into place. The day clothed itself again.

"Morning, fellas," he said, grin easy as sun through blinds. "Big day. Don't keep the Lord waiting."

Jeremiah pulled his pillow over his head and spoke into it. "Feels like the Lord could wait an hour."

"Mercies are new now," Scottie returned, not scolding. "Let's not miss 'em."

Tyler sat up, hair jagged with sleep, comic drifting from his lap to the floor. "Is murder an acceptable morning devotion if it's aimed at that bell?"

Scottie chuckled. "You can bring it to prayer and see how it lands."

Van swung his legs over the edge of the top bunk. The springs squealed as if they, too, had complaints about Monday.

THE BATHROOM WAS its own weather. Toothpaste foam sliding into sinks. Stalls clapping shut like cymbals. Showers running full-tilt and echoing off tile, steam fogging the scratched mirrors until faces turned into shapes. Van stayed at the sinks with his washcloth and soap, deliberate, slow. He washed wrists, neck, the back of his knees with a care that read as fastidious if you didn't know what it was. He kept his back to the showers and answered every "move it, man" with a quiet "one sec."

"Shelton," Jeremiah said, hip-checking him sideways and grabbing the neighboring sink. "You got a date with a mirror?"

"Yep. She's kinder than most," Van said, and made himself smile.

Breakfast was rubber eggs and a biscuit that needed forgiveness. The line inched. The mess hall hummed. Scottie sat at the head of their table, hands folded over his Bible even while they ate, posture relaxed like somebody who had learned to breathe on a hill. He tapped Van's tray once with a knuckle when the boy stared at it too long. "Fuel," he said. "Hill's not getting shorter."

Then the climb.

The staircase cut the green in a white scar—stone risers baked pale and unrelenting, the kind of steps that took half your breath when you looked at them and the other half when you started. They moved in a river of bodies and chatter, three across if no one minded bumping shoulders.

"Room inspections before lunch!" a counselor called. "Sheets tight, Bibles visible, trunks shut!"

"Bibles visible," Jeremiah said under his breath. "Like God misplaces them otherwise."

Tyler shook his head. "It's about honoring the space."

"Bless this neatly folded sock drawer," Jeremiah muttered, but a grin tugged his mouth.

Scottie fell in beside them for a stretch, red polo dark at the collar. "Quick check after breakfast," he said. "Not hotel-perfect. Just respectful." He let the word sit. "Canteen opens after lunch. If you blew your snack money on Monday, start praying for loaves and fishes."

Van's mouth moved before he could stop it. "Do they take miracles at the register?"

Scottie laughed; something unclenched in Van's chest at the sound.

THE CHAPEL at the ridge crown wore light well. Windows lifted it in and laid it across polished wood, across bent heads, across hymnals stacked and waiting. They slid into the row Scottie had kept open near the front: Jeremiah on one side of Van, Colby on the other, his shoulder an honest weight against Van's.

"Didn't think we'd end up up front," Colby whispered, breath edged in soap. "Everybody can see us."

"Guess we'll have to behave," Van murmured. He meant the joke; he felt the truth under it.

The band found their chord; the room followed. **"Blessed Assurance."** Arms lifted; some swayed; some mouthed; some belted like they'd been waiting to be asked to be loud all week. Van let his lips move. His mind kept catching on splinters— Colby's earlier line, the way Scottie's humming had felt like a kindness, his grandmother's voice from some deep shelf urging him to hold on to faith when the floor tilted.

The pastor's word for the week was **purification**. It landed in Van's lap like a hot coin—too small to hold, too bright to ignore. He pressed the corner of the bulletin into his thumb until the paper gave. When he glanced sideways, Colby was already looking—not bold, not pleading—simply there, as if asking a question that didn't fit in a prayer.

"Amen," the room breathed in one voice. Van said it, too, quiet and late.

THEY CIRCLED in the patchy shade near the dorms, grass still damp enough to darken the hems of shorts. Scottie sat cross-legged, Bible open, pages feathered with years. "This is our time," he said. "Honest, not polished. God's not scared of our questions."

Van looked up at that. *Even doubts.* The words felt like a door that opened in a place he'd been told was wall.

Scottie read, steady: *Trust in the Lord with all thine heart; and lean not unto thine own understanding.* He let the quiet do half the work. "Hard part's right there," he said, tapping the margin with his thumb. "We want to lean on what we know we feel. Faith asks for surrender."

The verse pricked Van. If not his own understanding—what else did he have? The tug toward Colby. The heat-and-shame mix from this morning's glimpse. The thousand sermons that said desire meant danger. His grandmother's soft counsel to listen for God in small spaces.

"Thoughts?" Scottie asked.

Tyler straightened. "It means obey the Bible even when it's hard."

"Good," Scottie said warmly.

Jeremiah flipped a pebble. "Maybe don't think it to death. Just... do church stuff 'til it sticks."

Scottie chuckled. "There's a word for that somewhere."

His eyes returned to Van, not pinning, offering room. "What about you?"

Van swallowed. The truth jammed in his throat. *I'm scared, I don't know how to stop what I feel, I can't tell if I'm breaking or being remade.* "Maybe it means believing God knows better than I do," he said at last. "Even when... it feels impossible."

Scottie nodded once, eyes soft. "That's honest." He closed the Bible with his palm resting on it like an anchor. "Faith grows best in the places we don't have tidy answers."

They bowed heads. Scottie prayed short and clean. Van kept his eyes on the ground a beat longer after amen, as if the dirt might answer faster than heaven.

As they stood, Jeremiah's shoulder brushed his. "You get real serious when Lane talks faith," he whispered, smirk low. "Trying to impress somebody?"

Van elbowed him back, light as he could manage. "Shut up, Jere."

Scottie clapped his hands once, not loud. "Breakfast—before the eggs die a second time."

THE CANTEEN'S bell jingled like it had been wired to optimism. A window unit rattled a lukewarm mercy into the room. A hand-lettered sign read: **MODESTY IN LINE. CHARITY AT THE REGISTER. NO IOUs.** Ms. Barb presided with sprayed hair and a name tag that had seen some summers.

"Two MoonPies and a Cheerwine," Seth announced. "And wisdom, if it's on special."

"Full price," Ms. Barb said. "And it doesn't come in grape."

Jeremiah leaned on a rack of sunflower seeds. "Van? MoonPie diplomacy?"

"I'm good," Van lied. Everything in the cooler looked like cold apology. Scottie's *respectful* still rang in his head for reasons that had nothing to do with snacks.

Ms. Barb thunked a small crate onto the counter. "Mail call! Miller, Ortiz, Porter, Shelton—who's my Shelton?"

Van's hand was up before he'd decided to raise it. She passed him a stiff white card with his name looped like ribbon. Aunt Shelia.

He stepped to the humming Coke cooler and opened it.

Baby, if the mountains feel loud, try listening between the sounds. That's where truth sits. Proud of you. Go easy on yourself—hard days count too. — Aunt Shelia.

A pressed dogwood fell out—spring pressed flat and kept.

He slid it into the back of his notebook like a secret he had permission to keep.

Jeremiah drifted close, not crowding. "Good news?"

"Yeah." Van didn't add the part about a single sentence being enough to carry an afternoon.

Across the room, Colby told a story to two boys from another church, hands drawing arcs. Each time he said *God showed up*, they nodded like they'd been there.

AS THE HEAT softened toward evening, the boys arranged themselves around a crooked picnic table under a buzzing floodlight. Colby sprawled with one leg hooked, laughter easy; Seth dealt cards with flourish he hadn't earned; Jeremiah sipped a Sprite and let his hat brim cast his eyes in shade.

Van hovered at the post, half in, half out of the light. They hadn't asked him to sit; they hadn't told him to go. That was how it was now—enough space to feel unwelcome without anyone naming it.

"You coming in," Colby called, "or just lurking like you're about to murder us?"

"Just got here," Van said.

"Leave him," Seth snorted. "He's on his poet thing."

Colby cut him a look. "Chill." It cost him a smirk and his place in the next joke, and he let it.

"We're playing bullshit," Seth said. "Winner gets first dibs on the sodas."

"Wild stakes," Van deadpanned.

Jeremiah flicked a glance up, met Van's eyes, looked away.

Van considered sliding onto the bench, muscle into the old rhythm, laugh at the old beats. His skin itched at the thought. "Nah. I'm good."

Colby's brow gathered. "You good, though? You've been... weird."

"Just tired," Van said.

"Soft," Seth muttered, eyes on the deck.

Jeremiah said nothing.

Van turned before someone decided to save him or to make fun of saving him. Laughter rose behind him, bright and easy. It didn't crack without him in it.

DEVOTIONS in the dorm ran quiet. Scottie read something short about the difference between noise and voice, then let the room breathe. When the overhead flicked off, the hall threw a pale rectangle across brick. A fan clicked—click... click... click—like a machine trying to catch up to itself.

"Rounds," Scottie said, more habit than warning. He checked the door latch and the cracked window, set his Bible on his knee but didn't open it—just rested his hand on the cover as if to feel it beating.

Van lay on his side, eyes open to the thin light. He slipped the pressed dogwood deeper into his notebook. *Between the sounds*, Aunt Shelia had written. He tried to listen there. Footsteps faded down the corridor. Someone coughed. Outside, a moth threw itself again and again against the screen and kept trying.

THE FLOODLIGHT'S circle fell behind him; the gravel thinned to dirt; the dirt softened into a floor of pine needles that held weight without telling anyone. The woods weren't exactly off-limits. They simply weren't advertised. Perfect.

The air back here tasted different. Sap and loam and the thin metal of evening sliding in. A log sat between two pines, edges going to sponge with rot but dry enough at the top to take a boy and a notebook.

Van sat. He didn't order the forest to be silent; it knew better than that. It hummed with little lives—leaf-shifts, twig ticks, a branch reporting its own small break. The kind of sound that wrapped instead of pressed.

He pulled the notebook. Bent corners. Warp from being the bottom layer of too many bags. He uncapped the pen with his teeth and found the last blank page.

No prompt. Just paper.

The first lines came jagged, like the pen was catching on the day:

I don't think I'm broken.

But I don't think I'm ready.

They're all learning how to belong.

I'm learning how to disappear.

That's not the same thing.

He paused. A breeze lifted the page as if to read it and kept going. He wrote one more line.

I don't want to be normal.

I just want to be real.

The tip of the pen throbbing in his fingers matched his pulse for a few beats. It didn't feel brave. It didn't fix anything. It just sounded true when nothing else did.

He capped the pen. Set the notebook on the log beside him. Tilted his head and watched the last thin orange threads caught high in the needles.

He didn't want to run. Not from this, anyway. He let the forest's steady unbothered breathing become the shape of the moment and sat inside it until the bell that had ripped the morning hung quietly against its frame and the day let go of him, one finger at a time.

CHAPTER 7
UNSTEADY GROUND

The bell clanged before the sun cleared the ridge, its hollow cry spilling down the valley and rattling the thin dorm windows. Van rolled deeper into his blanket and wished it would muffle more than sound. The notebook in his bag had taken last night's words and made them heavy—truths that felt like confessions even with no one to hear them.

Jeremiah was already up, stretching like a cat, hair pointing in six directions. "Morning, sunshine," he said, tossing a sock that smacked Van's shoulder.

Tyler lined his toothbrush and soap exactly parallel on the shelf, his bunk corners tight enough to salute. Scottie, somehow pressed and ready, leaned in the doorway with his whistle catching a line of light, grin wide. "Up and at it, fellas. Breakfast waits for no one, and neither do stairs."

Van muttered something into the pillow about stairs not being biblical, then swung his legs over the edge.

The climb to the mess hall felt like moving through a magnifying glass. Heat pooled on every step. Jeremiah bounded two at a time. Tyler huffed. Scottie's long stride didn't break.

Van kept his eyes down and counted—seventeen to the first landing, thirty-one to the second—because counting was easier than thinking.

Syrup and powdered eggs fogged the mess hall air. Trays clattered. Chairs scraped. Colby sat two tables over with Seth and a couple of girls from another church, laughter bright as if the room were lit from his chair. Van froze, just long enough to see the flash of that smile before Colby glanced over and tossed him a quick, almost-secret smirk. *I remember.* The next second he leaned in toward the girl like she was the center of gravity.

The stone in Van's stomach sank a little more.

Scottie slid into the seat across from him. "Eat," he said gently, nodding at Van's untouched eggs. "Full day." He didn't push; he just set a grape jelly beside Van's plate like a small mercy and went back to chewing.

They reported to the chapel's back lot with rollers and a case of paint labeled Camp Cardinal Red, which looked, to Jeremiah, "suspiciously like ketchup." A deacon set the rules in a single sentence—"Smooth coats, no drips; drips are sloth, sloth is sin"—and left them with the sun.

They painted into a silence made of squeaking rollers and the soft click of bristles on wood. Tyler worked like a jeweler, exact and close. Seth painted his forearm by accident and kept it like a joke. Colby grabbed end pieces and moved fast, efficient. Scottie checked the edges, knelt to swipe away a run before it found a home.

"Good," he said to Van, watching the roller's line. "Don't fight the grain. Work with it."

Van dragged a slow, steady coat and watched red fill the weathered boards. For once the instruction made sense—stop forcing; follow.

The morning shoved them from one thing to the next—relay races across grass that greened their knees, devotion circles under pines while cicadas sang a second gospel, water breaks that turned into jokes and then back into breaths. In the Rec Hall, rows of chairs faced a whiteboard: **PURITY = POWER**, and Mrs. Harper handed out a packet titled "Guardrails."

"Temptation is not sin," she said, voice kind and crisp. "Agreement is."

Her metaphors ran on cliff roads and good brakes. Some boys looked relieved, like a map had finally been drawn. Van watched a beetle throw itself, again and again, at the screen door and be flung back by what it couldn't see.

Beside him, Jeremiah sat unusually still, jaw working like he had a tough piece of candy he refused to spit out.

On the way out, Mrs. Harper pressed a folded paper into Colby's hand. "Verses for focus," she said. "You've got leadership in you." Colby glowed and tried not to let it show; Van looked away before the heat in his chest could name itself.

The bells called them to the chapel again. Voices rose until the rafters hummed and hands went up like they were reaching for a shelf. Van mouthed the words and felt... nothing. It wasn't defiance; it was distance. Like the tide had come in for everyone else and left his stretch of shore untouched.

At lunch, Jeremiah leaned into his shoulder with a joke about the line moving like molasses. Van laughed on cue. His eyes still slid toward Colby—who wasn't looking at him, and then was, a small smile flicked across the space like a match and gone. *I remember. But it's over.* The message stung and soothed in the same breath. Jeremiah noticed the flicker and let his shoulder linger against Van's an unnecessary second, his whispers closer than they needed to be. It wasn't bold; it was *almost*, and almosts were everywhere.

Youth choir ran "Come Thou Fount" in the late afternoon. A girl with a dark braid poured the melody like clean water; the alto wrapped the room. Colby stood in the tenor clump, not the best singer but the most intent, reading the notes like a map he meant to learn. Jeremiah didn't sing; he leaned on the back pew and watched more than he listened. Van let the harmony find him. For three verses, not thinking counted as grace.

Twilight pooled violet at the chapel steps. The camp gathered for vespers—just a guitar and songs everyone knew by heart. Scottie's voice rode along, steady. "Share a verse if you've got one," he said when the last chord faded. "Or a sentence. Doesn't need to be shiny."

Tyler recited a psalm, bright and exact. Seth said, "God's good," and didn't try to make it funny. Colby cleared his throat. "I... felt God painting," he said, flushing at his own admission. "Not about the paint. Just... doing the thing in front of me and not making it about me."

"Pastor Colby," Seth stage-whispered, earning a couple of snickers.

Colby shrugged, took the loss of cool, and didn't defend himself. Van tucked Aunt Shelia's sentence back into his pocket and held it like a warm coin: *listen between the sounds.*

By evening service, Van felt thin-skinned. The choir surged; beams seemed to tremble. Hands lifted. Faces tilted. Two rows up, Colby's profile held the light—the strong line of jaw, the open hands. Van stared at the shape of surrender and felt the particular ache of being left behind by something you still wanted.

Back in the dorm, the day came down in pieces. Tyler compared blisters like medals. Jeremiah lobbed easy jokes, fishing for a last laugh. Scottie reminded them of morning devotionals and thumbs-up checked the window latch. Van stared at the ceiling and breathed the thick stew of sweat and soap.

Outside, laughter rolled. Inside, the space where he and Colby used to live felt wider than the valley. Jeremiah's nearness buzzed. Scottie's steadiness lingered. But it was the shape of Colby's absence—sharp, deliberate—that pressed hardest on Van's chest.

He turned onto his side and watched the crack in the ceiling resolve into a small river again. He thought about paint settling into grain, about guardrails that made sense on paper and not in blood, about a smile tossed across a cafeteria and the way a single glance could keep you hanging from a thread.

For the first time, he let himself consider that the thread might already have snapped.

If it had, he didn't know what to do with the pieces in his hands. He only knew they were real. And he was tired of pretending they weren't.

CHAPTER 8

ALTAR CALLS AND ULTIMATUMS

B y midweek the days had melted together, stitched from the same cloth—whistle at dawn; showers and teeth; blankets folded to regulation squares; Scottie's voice carrying above the din, warm and unbothered: "Joy comes in the morning, fellas—let's go find it."

Breakfast buzzed—trays clacking, chairs scraping, hymns leaking thinly from ceiling speakers like a reminder not to forget who you were meant to be. Pancakes Monday. Grits Tuesday. Powdered eggs no matter what you prayed for. Then chapel. Then small groups. Then service. Then more chapel. Smiles at the right beats. Amens in the right places. Even laughter seemed scheduled.

Van played where he had to. Under it, the strain tightened.

Colby seemed to rise under the weight that pressed everyone else down. He sat forward in the pew, Bible open, pencil moving, hand up first when "Who will pray?" floated into the air. When a verse started, he finished it without looking, voice steady. Seth rode shotgun on his revival, echoing "Yes, Lord," too loud. Jeremiah held his corner a half-step away from it all, ready with a joke when the room got too tight, but quieter when the silence landed.

An hour before the guest preacher, a seam of rain gathered over the ridge and then changed its mind, leaving the air swollen and restless. Hymnals propped open the chapel doors. Bulletins turned into fans that didn't cool anything. Scottie moved the aisle with paper cups, pressing one into Van's hand. "Drink," he murmured, as if thirst were a solvable sin. Van sipped and felt foolish for how much it felt like kindness.

Mrs. Harper leaned across the aisle and touched Colby's elbow, said something short that made him stand a little taller. Van looked away before it could land.

The preacher from Georgia came heavy and certain, sweat already jeweling his forehead. His voice filled the rafters on the first breath—deep, rolling, the kind of sound that made even the windows want to listen. He painted hell in colors that didn't need a projector. He listed the ruin by name—liars, adulterers, fornicators, backsliders, sodomites—and sent each word out like a stone. Van pressed his palms flat on his thighs and took the throw. The preacher didn't know his name. It didn't matter.

Around him, motion. Kleenex pulled; Bibles clutched; someone sobbing in hitching gulps two rows back. Van thought of his father's warnings, of pew whispers, of every sideways glance that taught a boy to fold himself small. He thought of Scottie's Bible, swollen with ink and use, and how different a book could sound depending on who held it.

Then the voice dropped to a near whisper. "Don't wait. Hell's mouth is hungry. Heaven's gate is open. Come."

The pianist slid into "Just As I Am," soft and trembling. Counselors took their places at the front, palms laced, scanning.

Colby stood before the second verse. No glance sideways, no pause. He went like a boy headed toward a finish line only he could see—head high, shoulders set. Seth followed and clapped him once on the back like an amen with hands. Feet scraped; aisles filled; the front became a small forest of bent shoulders.

Van didn't move. His chest thudded hard enough to feel it in his wrists. He watched a counselor settle a hand between Colby's shoulder blades. He watched tears leave clean lines on Colby's face and didn't know if they washed him or only showed where the salt had run. Whatever had lived unnamed between them was being rewritten in public light, not with cruelty, but with a kind of goodness that didn't have room for him.

He wanted to run. He sat still.

"Amen," the preacher said finally, and the word broke like a starter's pistol. The last chord hung and fell. Up front, counselors and kids rocked back on their heels like swimmers coming up from a deep pool, blinking, breathing, laughing through tears. Some turned to look at the altar on their way out like you look back at a room something happened to you in.

Van felt both unchanged and skinned.

Jeremiah hadn't moved either. He sank deeper, hands jammed into pockets, leg bouncing to a rhythm that didn't match the hymn. Van stole a glance and caught the tight line of his mouth. No tears. No bowing. No folded hands. Later, when whispers floated—*saved, rededicated*—Jeremiah tilted toward Van, voice flat enough to cut. "Guess some of us are just damned, huh."

The words weren't aimed at Van. They flew past him and stuck in the pulpit. Maybe in Jeremiah's own front pew back home. Van had no answer that wouldn't make it worse.

Back at the dorm, before anyone could climb into bunks or into a version of the story that fit better, Scottie called a circle. He didn't stand over them. He sat cross-legged on the concrete, eye level.

"Big night," he said. "Feels like a wave. If you rode it 'til you couldn't breathe, if you got pulled under, if you stayed on the shore—God isn't taking attendance."

Seth blinked. "Aren't we supposed to... go? You know. *Go.*"

"You're supposed to tell the truth," Scottie said, voice even. "If tonight was your truth, let it be that. If it wasn't, don't fake it to make me proud. I won't be."

Colby's jaw worked, not with anger—effort. Van wanted to say *thank you* and had no words that didn't feel like a trick.

They broke. The room rearranged itself into smaller orbits.

Colby paced the short aisle between bunks, eyes still bright, words coming fast. "I feel—different," he said, searching for a door that matched the feeling. "I don't want to mess around anymore. I want to be better. Live right. Be who God wants."

Seth nodded too hard, knocking his shoulder into a bedpost. "Man, you were on fire."

Van sat on his mattress and watched the scuff on the floor by his shoe. Colby kept going, the sentences tightening. "I can't waste time on stuff that drags me down. I need to cut it. All of it."

The words didn't come like knives. They landed like rules, and rules still bruise. *All of it* rang against Van's ribs and kept ringing.

Jeremiah leaned on the wall, arms crossed, expression plain as drywall. Only his eyes moved—one quick flick toward Van that said *I heard it too* and then gave nothing else away.

Scottie stood finally, Bible in hand, and drew a line under the night with calm. "All right, fellas. Let's pray it out and sleep like people who get another morning."

The prayer flowed—gratitude, guardrails, help us hear— and Van missed most of it, his own thoughts too loud. When *amen* came, it felt like a period. The night, however, didn't end. It just lay down beside him and stared at the ceiling.

The next afternoon, Scottie dropped a stack of index cards

and a fistful of pens on the nearest bunk. "Write home. Or to yourself. Or to the kid you needed to be last year. Just a line. Be kind."

Tyler printed neat and small. Seth drafted three and drew a bicep on each like a signature. Colby bowed his head over his words like the right sentence might appear if he clenched hard enough.

Van stared at the blank until the pen bled a dark dot in the corner. Then he wrote:

Aunt Shelia,

I'm okay. I painted a table. I sang a verse. I didn't walk up front. I don't know if that's failure or honesty. You said listen between the sounds. I'm trying. I can hear something. I just don't know if it's me or God.

Love, V.

He didn't write that he tore up the first try. Or that he'd reached for *Grandma* out of habit and stopped, hand frozen over the G.

Scottie rubber-banded the stack. "Post goes at four," he said, like telling them mercy had a timetable and he planned to meet it.

Outside, thunder muttered somewhere that might have been the ridge or might have been inside Van's chest. Inside, the room went on smelling like soap and sweat and boys who were trying to become something—right, good, forgiven—without knowing what would be left over when they were done.

Van folded what he had left—truths he could say on paper, truths he couldn't say at all—and put them back where they'd be close enough to hear if they started speaking.

He didn't know what to do with Colby's new brightness or Jeremiah's dark quiet. He only knew the week had shifted the ground under all three of them, and the hill they were climbing wasn't just the one with the chapel on top.

CHAPTER 9

TESTING BOUNDARIES

The next afternoon, camp loosened its grip like a fist relaxing by degrees. A block on the schedule read **FREE TIME** in fat black letters—as if the directors had remembered that even the most eager Baptist teenager needed a breath that wasn't measured in verses. No chapel. No scripture drills. No counselors pacing aisles with the posture of watchmen. Just sunlight, a little wind off the lake, and the sound of a hundred kids deciding what to do with themselves when no one told them how.

The valley rang with it. Boys spilled onto the lower field in loose packs; a football arced end-over-end, skimming the hot air; sneakers skittered dust; a plastic cone toppled and rolled until a tree root stopped it. Under the pines, the girls settled on the needle-soft ground and made quick work of each other's hair—elastic bands between teeth, fingers dividing and weaving, laughter popping like corn. Every few minutes a boy tried not to stare and failed spectacularly.

Van stood on the lip of it all, arms crossed, back warm against the sun-baked stones edging the field. Freedom, in a place built on rules, came with a lot of witnesses. He wasn't sure what to do with that. The whistle lay quiet somewhere for the first time all day and he missed it in a way that irritated him. Structure made decisions for you. Free time wanted you to confess what you actually wanted.

Colby wanted a football and a spotlight. He was already barefoot, shirt tossed into a pile, running a route that needed no diagram. Seth jogged beside him, loud as ever, palms cracking against Colby's back after each catch like they were trying to clap the heat out of the day. They looked like brothers for hire— same laugh, same easy ownership of space, like the world had already drafted them and fitted them with the right jerseys.

Jeremiah stayed at the edge of the game and at the center of attention anyway, cap brim low, hands in pockets. He called plays no one followed, shouted "hold" when nobody was, booed a phantom ref. When a pass went wild and skidded to his sneakers, he toe-tapped it back with a lazy flick and grinned like he'd done more than he meant.

A counselor loped past, whistle bouncing against his chest like a heartbeat. "Not your thing?" he called, not unkind.

Van gave him a smile that didn't show teeth. "Pacing myself."

"Smart," the counselor said, like Van had passed a test, and kept jogging.

He sat on the low wall and let the afternoon press its warm weight onto his shoulders. The camp looked alive from here— two boys arguing about whether a Frisbee counts as a sport, a circle of girls practicing harmonies for evening service, Scottie down by the equipment shed counting jump ropes back into a bin and letting three extra go uncounted because mercy was quicker. This was supposed to be free. Van felt anything but.

By midafternoon the herd moved downhill in a long, loose line pulled by heat and rumor: **Lake** in block letters on a map no one needed. The water lay green as a bottle under the sun, ringed in pines that held a little shade like a secret. A dock pushed out into the shallows, boards bleached gray and softened at the edges by years of wet feet. A lone rope tied to a post dreamed of being a swing and wasn't.

"Modesty, folks," a counselor sang, clapping. "Boys in shirts until the water; girls in one-pieces. We will enforce modesty in every splash." He smiled like he was joking and wasn't.

Van trailed the pack, towel slung over his shoulder, taking careful inventory of exits, shadows, where the deeper water slipped from green to darker green. The thought of un-layering with a hundred eyes around made his stomach turn a slow circle. He'd learned long ago that boys made quiet comparisons in louder rooms.

Colby took the moment and made it his. He sprinted the run-up and cut clean into the lake in a tight arc, a sheet of water lifting off the surface and throwing a rainbow back at the sun. He surfaced with a whoop, hair slicked back, shoulders shiny. Seth cannonballed after, soaking a dozen shrieks at the rail, then crowed like he'd invented gravity.

Jeremiah walked the last few planks, toeing his sandals off one at a time. He peeled his shirt away in a single motion and tossed it toward the pile without checking where it landed. Leaner than Colby, all lines and angles, sun-browned and careless, he cut a smooth slip into the water and vanished. He surfaced, swiped water from his face, and glanced up long enough to find Van, smirk already there like it had been waiting.

Van folded his own shirt like he could hide inside neatness and set it on his towel; the folding felt silly and necessary. He sat on the edge first and let his feet remember cold. Then he slid in, the water taking him in one steady breath. It wrapped him in a way the air never did. He stayed near the rail where he could touch bottom and pretend it was on purpose.

"Jump, Shelton!" Colby called, slicking hair, grin bright. "Don't be a grandma."

"Save the grandmas," Van said, and smiled, and slipped under to save his face.

The lake filled with boys proving buoyancy: wrestling near the ladder, racing nowhere, flipping girls off floats and getting yelled at by the counselor who laughed after he yelled. A hymn drifted from the shore where a small cluster of girls practiced tight harmonies and ignored boys on purpose. Van floated on his back and let the water drum his ears until voices sank to a hum.

Jeremiah cut past close enough for his shoulder to brush Van's—the kind of touch easy to chalk up to water. "Relax," he said low, eyes forward. "Nobody's keeping score."

Van wanted to believe him and didn't. Here, everyone kept some score—of speed, of jokes, of who meant what to whom.

They sprawled on the dock in a row when the whistle bought them a few minutes before "clear the water." Sun ran a line down the wet planks. Someone started **two truths and a lie**; someone else accused all the lies of being boring and played anyway.

"Truth," Seth said, rolling to an elbow. "I once ate six hot dogs in one sitting."

"Lie," Jeremiah said without looking up. "Low number."

Colby flicked a spray of water toward Van. "Shelton. Two and a half truths."

Van shielded his face and surprised himself by playing without dread. "Okay. I fell asleep under the bleachers at a JV game once. I can play 'Heart and Soul' with one hand. And... I mailed my first letter to myself."

Jeremiah turned his head. "Which one's the lie?"

"You pick," Van said.

Colby squinted like a coach reading a defense. "Bleachers is true. You're that tired."

"Rude," Van said, but he let the smile stay.

"I'm stuck on the last one," Jeremiah said. "To yourself?"

"Why not," Van answered. "Somebody's gotta answer."

No one had a joke ready for that. The dock creaked; the lake nibbled at the pilings. The whistle blew; they slid back into water with less noise than they'd made climbing out. For a second, the silence that followed felt like a real thing you could hold.

By the time the counselors blew the final long note to clear the lake, they'd invented four more ways to be boys and turned away from three of them because a whistle somewhere in the backs of their skulls still ran the schedule. The last of the sunlight flipped coins on the water. They lay out again, steaming like lizards, giddy on tired and too much sun.

Seth started it. Seth always started it.

"Bet none of you can swim across without stopping," he said, grin showing teeth.

Colby sat up like a string had been pulled. "Bet I beat you there and back."

They hooted and made a show of stretching that helped exactly no one. They dove. They came up. They didn't cross the lake because a counselor's shout pinned them to their side at the halfway mark, and they took the walk of shame back to the ladder laughing like they'd planned that too.

The dares shifted rule sets. Who could hold breath the longest. Who could cut the cleanest dive. Who could cannonball biggest and not get called out. Boys broke themselves into little records on purpose.

On the warm boards, Seth leaned in with the grin he saved for ideas that set off alarms. "Tonight," he said. "After lights. Mess hall. Sodas."

It wasn't about soda and everyone knew it. It was about touching the electric fence to make sure it was on.

"Easy," Colby said, and the way he said it proved it wasn't. "We're in."

Jeremiah looked over the line of his shoulder at Van. "You in, Shelton?"

The question carried more than fizz. It carried the look from the cafeteria, the new lines Colby had spoken last night, the part of Van that wanted proximity even if it came dressed up as bad ideas. Colby's eyes were on him. Seth's grin widened. Jeremiah's mouth didn't move, but his attention did.

"Yeah," Van heard himself say. "Sure."

The cheer that followed felt brighter than it deserved to. He couldn't tell if what rose in his chest was dread or relief. Maybe both.

Lights-out baked the dorm into one long quiet complaint. At 11:10, a flashlight beam licked the hall and vanished. Somewhere in another room, someone snored in a rhythm that would have gotten applause if it hadn't been two doors down.

"Canteen," Seth whispered into the ceiling. "Ready?"

Jeremiah slid bare feet into sneakers. Colby stood already, hair combed by habit, not vanity. Van tied laces in the dark and told himself this wasn't rebellion; it was proximity, and that word, while ridiculous, fit. They ghosted into the stairwell: Seth first because he needed to be; Colby right behind because he needed to prove he could be; Jeremiah's hand stamping Van's shoulder once—there / not there.

At the bottom they melted into shadow as a counselor's keys chimed a note and went past. The mess hall porch loomed like a ship's prow, stairs yawning, Coke machine glowing red and vacant like a friendly lie. Seth pressed his ear to the vending machine like he could hear mercy humming inside it. "Unplugged," he whispered, offended.

"Guess we're not the first," Jeremiah said.

Colby pulled the porch fridge handle and found it locked. His breath eased out through his nose. "We could go back," he said too quickly, and Van heard the truth under it: *He wanted to go back. He needed to be the boy who did.*

Keys again—closer this time. They became azaleas with the practiced speed of boys who'd learned hiding as a language: flattened in the green, thorns politely ignoring bare shins. A flashlight combed the porch and slid, the leaves teaching light how to be leaf-colored.

"Back," Colby breathed when the beam swung away. It trembled just enough for anyone who loved him to hear.

They walked in the same order, but slower. At the stairwell Seth tried a laugh that landed as breath. Jeremiah bumped Van's shoulder for no reason he explained. Back in their bunks, the not-sodas tasted exactly like safety and pride, which is to say, like nothing. Van stared at the ceiling and waited for his pulse to remember how to be a metronome.

The air clung to skin. Boys rotated on mattresses like rotisserie chickens. A fan clicked out of time and did almost nothing. Colby found Van by the door with a look that asked for a quick word and got one.

"About earlier," he said, eyes skimming the room and dropping. "Just... don't take it too far, okay? This stuff—it's fun until it isn't. We're here for a reason. I'm trying to..." He stopped and hunted up a phrase. "Get right." He didn't look smug when he said it. He looked scared he might not.

The words weren't knives. They were guardrails. But even guardrails bruise if you bounce against them enough. **Don't mess this up** sat quiet at the base of them. Van nodded because he understood, and because *I don't know what counts as too far anymore* wasn't a thing he could say to the boy setting distances so carefully.

He slipped into the hallway for water when the room's breath felt like something alive. The metal bubbler screamed when he pressed the paddle; he winced and drank anyway, the cold slapping him back into place.

Scottie sat on the floor under the **FIRE EXTINGUISHER** sign like the night had asked him to keep it company. His back rested against brick, long legs out, Bible beside his hip but closed. He lifted two fingers in a quiet hello. "Can't sleep either?"

"Can't turn my head off," Van said, and the plainly teenage sound of it made him want to apologize.

"Comes with having one," Scottie said, as if he'd invented the brain. He tipped his chin toward the fountain. "Hydrate. Think slow."

"How?" Van asked, and intended it as a joke. It came out honest.

"Same way you painted that table," Scottie said. "Don't fight the grain."

"That a verse?" Van asked, because it felt like one.

"It's a craft lesson," Scottie said. "But if you need it to be a verse, I'll write a reference in the margin." His smile didn't press for anything. He let the quiet sit there like a chair for Van to use or not.

"Thanks," Van said, and meant it. He didn't say *I don't know how to be in this skin in this place*. The hallway didn't require that much.

Back in the dim, he slid his notebook out from under his pillow. The page took the light like it had been waiting without comment. He wrote three words on a clean line: **Think. Slow. Breathe.** He underlined *breathe* twice like a teacher might check a problem and finally got it right. Then he obeyed his own handwriting until the rush under his ribs stepped back half a foot.

Something shifted above him. Jeremiah slid to the edge of his bunk, then to the floor, movements quiet in the way of boys who'd learned how not to wake a room. He pulled his knees up and leaned back against brick, sat down in Van's patch of dark without asking if it was taken. He didn't touch him. He didn't talk. He watched the same mess of shadow like it might sort itself.

Van wrote like that—fragments stacked at odd angles:

The weight of their expectations. The way Colby's words felt like a door closing softly, polite as a hotel. The silence that sits heavy and won't say its name.

The pen trembled once. He left the shake in the line. Jeremiah's breathing settled toward slow. He stayed. Didn't fill anything. Didn't leave. The quiet stretched between them, not tight enough to choke, not loose enough to waste.

It wasn't closeness. Not exactly. It wasn't distance either. It was a third thing he didn't have a name for yet, and sometimes naming came later.

When the dorm finally convinced itself to sleep, the sounds all ran together—rustle, cough, a soft laugh from down the hall, someone turning, the fan insisting on its wrong tempo. Outside, a whistle blew once because someone had to prove to the night that rules survived the dark. Van slid the notebook back under his pillow, unfinished words warm at his cheek. Across the aisle, Jeremiah shifted like a cloud re-arranging and went still.

Van lay awake in the soft grind of hush, chest tight with what he hadn't said—Colby's careful warning, Jeremiah's wordless nearness, the long space between the boy he was and the boy he was supposed to be. When sleep came, it tripped and stumbled on its way to him and didn't stay long.

Morning would come anyway, the bell pretending it had invented dawn. The schedule would stand at attention. The hill would still be there. The grain would run the way it ran, and he would try not to fight it, one small, slow breath at a time.

CHAPTER 10
THE WILDERNESS MILE

The bell ripped the morning open, and for once the sound didn't turn everyone toward the chapel. Clipboards waited by the mess hall doors; a crate of canteens clanged like small bells of their own; counselors checked lists and cinched straps.

"Wilderness hike, fellas," Scottie said, voice easy. "Five miles out, one night under the stars, five miles back. Enough to remember you've got legs. Enough to remember the world existed before loudspeakers."

Van weighed the pack Scottie handed him. It felt heavier than it looked—like most things at this camp. In the shade by the steps, Emmalee stood with her girls' unit, socks bunched at her ankles, ponytail crooked, trying to act braver than her eyes allowed. Millie Shelton's careful instructions lived in the tight fold of Emmalee's rolled T-shirt.

"You'll pass us on the service road," she told Van, chin high. "If I die, tell Mom I tried."

"You won't," Van said, and tugged her elastic straight. "Watch the roots. And pretend you like raisins."

Scottie gathered Room Fourteen by the map board. "Two

rules," he said, tapping the laminated trail with a knuckle. "First: stay inside the line. It's wider than it looks. Second: nobody carries their own misery alone. If you're tired, say tired. We'll share it." His hunter-green Bible peeked from his daypack like a habit.

They set out in a bright line—boys up front playing leaders until the first incline stole their swagger, Tyler counting switch-backs under his breath, Jeremiah hanging back with Van, kicking small stones into the brush. Colby moved with the first pod, frame easy, talking softly with a counselor from another church, nodding at whatever adult words good boys nod at—discipline, calling, purpose.

The heat came early, but the trail offered mercy in patches: a pine tunnel that smelled like sap and shade, a brook that asked them to balance on a row of stones like coins, a wide place where the sky pressed close and the hills folded and refolded like a map that didn't mind creases. Every few minutes, the line accordioned—boys bunching on a root, then stringing out again. Sneakers found rhythm; shoulders dropped; noise bled into the trees and came back thinner.

"Ten minutes," Scottie said at the first clearing, palming his watch. "Water and quiet. You don't have to be holy. You just have to be honest."

Van sank onto a slab of granite and tipped his canteen. Water ran cold and fat down his throat; he swallowed and felt every inch of it. He closed his eyes and let the silence do what it wanted. In the space between footsteps and wind, a line skimmed the top of his thoughts and stuck: *Enough for the day is enough.* He didn't know if that was scripture or Aunt Shelia or just what the rock wanted to say.

They started again. The trail rose.

At the second mile, the girls' unit crossed below on the service road, a flutter of color and complaint. Emmalee limped for drama and then limped for real when her heel rubbed raw. Van spotted her before she spotted him.

"Hey," he called down, kneeling at the lip of the bank. "Show me." She looked up with relief she tried to hide, and he came down the sandy slope like he'd rehearsed it. He knelt and peeled her sock back carefully. The blister was small and honest. Van wrapped it with the strip of moleskin Scottie had slipped him at breakfast and pretended he'd remembered it on his own.

Colby climbed down without being asked and handed Emmalee his extra water. "Only if you trade me that face for a brave one," he said lightly.

She sniffed and nodded. "I have two brave ones," she said, and tried one on. Colby grinned and took her empty cup; Emmalee beamed like she'd earned a ribbon.

Scottie watched from the ridge and didn't make a speech.

In the third mile the sky gathered itself into something and then let it go. A thin storm shouldered through the pines and shook loose a quick rain that darkened dust and cooled shoulders. Jeremiah slipped on a slick root and barked a laugh at himself that sounded like an apology no one asked him to make. Van reached without thinking and caught him by the elbow. The jolt ran up both their arms.

"Thanks," Jeremiah said, for once not turning it into a joke.

"You're welcome," Van said, and didn't move his hand for half a beat he hoped didn't show. He felt the warning under his ribs and let go.

They reached the campsite mid-afternoon—a bowl of earth ringed in laurel, a fire ring black with other weeks' stories, the lake a bright coin through the trees. Tents came out of duffels in bundles that made sense to some boys and not to others. Scottie let them puzzle and then stepped in just before frustration became drama.

"Corners to wind," he said, pinning a stake with his palm. "Don't fight the grain."

"Craft lesson," Van said before he could stop himself.

Scottie glanced up, amused. "It travels."

They cooked something that hoped to be dinner over a small, sensible flame. Seth burned the first hot dog black and declared it perfect; Tyler turned his like a safecracker with a dial. Colby took a quiet half-duty—collecting cups, handing napkins, washing his own fork without being asked. Van noticed the parts of goodness that didn't need an audience. It hurt and helped at the same time.

As dusk turned the trees purple, Scottie lifted a hand and the noise collapsed in a polite heap. "Two things," he said. "First, a silence. Ten minutes. Not a punishment. A gift. You can watch the lake think. It's better at it than most of us. Second, after that, you can speak a sentence if you want. Not a speech. A sentence."

The boys tried to smirk and couldn't get it to stick. The quiet came like a soft animal and sat down among them. Van watched the lake shrug off small wind. Somewhere a night bird called and waited for an answer. In the dark behind his ribs, the ache settled into a shape he could name for the length of a breath.

When Scottie said, "Okay," a few boys used their sentence. Tyler: "This is nicer than I thought." Seth: "I'm hungry again already." A kid from another church: "I want to be kinder when people aren't looking." Colby stared at the fire and said, "Thank you," as if the air could carry it where it needed to go. Van didn't speak. His sentence lived on paper.

Lights out in tents had a different weight than lights out in cinderblock. The night pressed down gentle but complete. Counselors took the first watch near the fire; a second set promised to relieve them. The lake kept its own counsel.

Sometime after the camp hushed, Jeremiah's whisper found Van through nylon. "Walk?"

"Where?" Van mouthed back, not ready to break anything.

"Just up to the ridge. Look at the lights," Jeremiah said. "You can see town."

They moved like boys who'd practiced leaving quietly. The ridge offered a ribbon of far, far away—pinprick lights like someone else's idea of home. The air tasted like iron and wet leaves. Jeremiah sat and pulled his knees up, arms looped around them, chin on forearms, the posture of a kid making himself smaller to be safer.

"What you said last night," Van began, careful. "About being damned."

Jeremiah chuckled with no joy in it. "Yeah, well. Pastor Lane makes it sound like the trap door's already open under my chair."

"He's your dad," Van said, as if that information were new.

"Exactly," Jeremiah said, not unkind. "He's never not the pastor. Even when he's the dad." He picked at a flake of bark and didn't look up. "I don't want to be saved *from* myself. I want to be safe *with* myself. They're not the same."

Van let the words sit where they landed. He thought of Scottie's "God isn't taking attendance," of Colby's "cut it out... all of it," of the way silence in the woods felt kinder than silence in a pew.

A footfall behind them. Scottie's outline eased out of tree shadow like he belonged to it. He didn't ask why they were out. He didn't make his voice bigger than it needed to be.

"Trail's easy to leave and hard to find again in the dark," he said. "Walk back with me."

They did. He didn't talk on the way. At the tent line he added, "Rules keep cabins safe. Truth keeps hearts safe. Work on both. Not just one." He tipped his head toward the fire, where another counselor rotated in and sat down with the relief of someone who'd earned the log.

In his sleeping bag, Van listened to the lake breathing and repeated the line he'd found on the rock earlier—*enough for the day is enough*—until his body believed him.

They woke to a sky the color of tin and coffee that tasted like penance. The trail back felt shorter because every return does, and longer because everyone's feet were tired. At the brook, Jeremiah paused and let Van step first. At the service road, Emmalee waved both arms like she'd never wave again and then pretended she was bored at having a brother.

Near the base of the hill, Van looked up through a break in the pines and saw the chapel roof cut a clean shape against the morning. It wasn't the only high place here. But it was the one with the bell.

He squared his shoulders and kept walking.

CHAPTER II
TESTIMONIES AND STONES

They hit the mess hall like a tide—mud-striped calves, hair pointing at the sky, smiles too big for faces that tired. The smell of tater tots and something calling itself barbecue wrapped them like a blanket no one wanted but everyone used. Ms. Barb rang the canteen bell twice for no reason and everyone cheered anyway.

"Write home goes at four," Scottie said, sliding the index-card stack onto their table like a small stack of chances. "Same rules—one line counts."

Van pulled his card closer and didn't write yet. He pocketed a grape jelly and ate it plain. The sugar hit and made promises it couldn't keep.

Afternoon rotated to **preparation**. The counselors called it "sharing time practice," which sounded harmless until you saw the whiteboard: **TESTIMONY NIGHT – TWO MINUTES**. Mrs. Harper clicked a marker and drew boxes like a flowchart—Before, Turning, Now.

"God likes clarity," she said, kind as ever. "So do your listeners." She handed Colby a packet she'd photocopied so many

77

times the clipart dove looked pixelated. "You've got a good word, son. Don't waste it."

Colby nodded too fast and then slowed his head to make it mean something. He thumbed the edge of the packet until the corner curled. Van watched from the second row and felt a door pull gently toward its frame.

Outside, the heat simmered. Emmalee's unit marched past with trash bags and tongs, a service project in motion—pick up what other people left behind. She spotted Van and then pretended she hadn't until she couldn't stand it. She broke rank, bounced to him, and pressed a folded note into his palm like contraband.

"From Mom - Ms Barb said the mail ran late." she whispered and ran back to her line.

Van unfolded the note. *Proud of you for the hike. Proud of you for helping your sister. Proud of you when you think you didn't do anything worth writing down. — M.* It wasn't poetry. It worked like one anyway.

Before evening chapel, the camp gathered by the lake for vespers with a new twist. A five-gallon bucket of smooth gray stones sat beside the guitar case. The counselor with the loudest shirts held one up.

"Pick a stone," he said. "If there's something you're laying down—fear, anger, old lies—name it, then throw it. If not, it's okay to hold it. Sometimes not letting go yet is honest."

Honesty, like water, moved the quick way among teenagers. They lined and bent, palms weighed the stones like fruit. Seth lobbed his with a baseball grunt and shouted, "Pride!" A shy kid whispered "shame" so quietly the water had to lean to hear it. Tyler tested three stones for flatness and finally let go of "comparing myself."

Colby stepped to the edge and held his a long time. He didn't say the word out loud. He threw hard, and the stone went far. The ripples kept expanding long after he stepped back. Mrs. Harper put a hand on his shoulder and pinched slightly, the way someone does when they're telling you you did a good job without making you look at them.

Jeremiah rolled his stone in his palm and then dropped it back into the bucket. "Not yet," he said when a counselor raised an eyebrow. The counselor nodded, which both surprised and steadied Van.

Van kept his, too. He didn't know what he would be naming if he threw it. He suspected the name would be wrong until he had a better one. He slipped it into his pocket and felt its round cool there like a promise not to rush.

Testimony night filled the chapel to the rafters. The band gave them a chorus and then sat down, and the microphone on the stand looked taller than usual. Counselors lined the front pew like hedges. Kids wiped palms on pants and waited to be brave.

They came in waves—simple and ragged and true. A girl from First Baptist whose mother had left in March said, "I felt lonely, and then I didn't." Two friends from the same youth group took turns like a duet—one speaking the before while the other mouthed the after with her. A boy Van didn't know cried all the way through without stopping and no one told him not to.

Colby walked to the front in that careful stride that said *don't trip* and *don't look away* at the same time. He didn't take his packet. He didn't need it anymore.

"I've been chasing the right words," he began, voice steady. "I thought if I got them in the right order, God would want me. But it turns out He wanted me messy, too." A small dry laugh. "I've had... distractions. Things that pull me." He chose his next words like stepping stones. "I asked for help letting go of what isn't God's for me. I don't know what that means for everything yet. I just know I'm saying yes where I can see it." He looked down as if it were easier to talk to the grain of the wooden lectern than to a room. "If I've pushed anybody away trying to figure that out, I'm sorry." He didn't look at Van. He didn't have to. The apology traveled anyway, whether or not it was meant as one.

"Amen," someone said, and meant it. Mrs. Haper dabbed her eye with a tissue like she wouldn't admit it later. Seth whooped and got shushed and grinned through the shush.

Van clapped. The sound felt like a thing he could give without tearing anything else. It still hurt. He wasn't sure it wasn't supposed to.

After the service, kids swarmed the side doors like they always did—congratulations as currency, arm squeezes as punctuation. In the back aisle, Pastor Lane materialized at Jeremiah's shoulder like a habit.

"Proud of you for coming, son," he said. The word *son* didn't soften anything.

Jeremiah's jaw ticked once. "I sat where I was," he said, neutral as a weather report.

Pastor Lane mouth pressed into a line that might have been a smile and might have been a gate. "The invitation's still there. You know where to find it."

"Yeah," Jeremiah said. "I do."

The pastor touched his shoulder—light, proprietary—and moved toward the next cluster of kids who needed pastoral gravity. Jeremiah didn't move until he had to. When he did, it was toward the outer doors, air, and Van.

"I'm not damned," he said, too softly to be dramatic. "I'm deciding."

"I know," Van said. He did.

The night broke into smaller circles—laughter on the steps, whispered retellings of the same stories to new ears, a guitar that refused to go to bed. Van found the bench by the flagpole because his feet did. The stone in his pocket warmed.

Scottie sat beside him without the ceremony of asking. He didn't carry his Bible this time. He held a Styrofoam cup that probably contained water and could have contained coffee.

"Good night to cry and not know why," he said.

Van huffed a laugh that had no meanness in it. "Good night to clap and not know if it hurts someone."

"Both can be true," Scottie said. "More often than not." He let the quiet run a few yards ahead. "When I was your age," he added, "I didn't go up front three nights in a row when everything in the room said I should. I went on a walk and told God I didn't like being bossed around by feelings that might not be His. He didn't mind. He met me anyway. On the walk. In the not-going."

Van let that unfold. "The altar isn't the only place God listens," he said, surprised to hear his own voice say it.

"Correct," Scottie said. "Sometimes the altar is a log by a fire. Sometimes it's a hallway fountain. Sometimes it's a five-mile trail where a boy helps his sister and doesn't write it down because it didn't feel like church."

Van swallowed around something that wasn't sadness. "What if I don't know what I'm supposed to throw? At the lake."

"Then don't throw it," Scottie said simply. "Set it down and see if it follows you. Things that aren't yours have a way of rolling away on their own."

They sat there until the mosquitoes convinced them to honor the hour. On the way back to the dorm, Van palmed the stone and felt its roundness press into his lifeline. At the threshold he placed it on the brick windowsill like a marker on a trail he could find again.

Inside, boys were still cataloging the night like sports

commentators. Seth re-enacted Colby's "I've had distractions" line with hand motions and got smacked with a pillow for it. Tyler shaved a curl off a pencil to calm down. Jeremiah lay on his bunk with his cap over his eyes and one ankle crossed over the other, an X that meant *no entry* and *not asleep* both at once.

Van slid his notebook out. The page waited. He wrote:

Tonight, I didn't throw anything. I set it down. If it's not mine, it'll roll.

He pictured the lake taking the weight of a hundred small griefs and keeping all their secrets. He pictured the hill with the chapel on top and the other hill that needed no building.

The fan clicked the wrong tempo. The hall light threw a long rectangle across the floor. The bell slept. Morning would wake it, because morning always did.

Van closed the notebook and slid it under his pillow. Between the sounds, he could hear something steady that belonged to him—small, real, enough for the day.

CHAPTER 12

BETWEEN THE LIVING
AND THE LEAVING

The doctor was a small man with thinning hair and glasses that kept sliding down his nose. His white coat looked a size too big, sleeves swallowing his wrists as he stood with a clipboard pressed to his chest like a shield outside the ICU doors.

"She's stable for now," he said carefully. "The stroke was significant. We won't know the full extent until—"

"She's dying, isn't she?" Van's father boomed, loud enough to make two nurses glance over the counter.

The doctor blinked. "No, sir. I didn't say—"

"You doctors never say it plain." Color climbed Van's father's neck. "She raised five children without asking for help, and now you stutter while she lies hooked to machines!"

"Daddy—" Van's mother reached for his sleeve.

He yanked free. "Don't 'Daddy' me. He's telling us nothing while Mama's slipping away!"

Aunt Leslie stepped forward, lips tight, voice polished. "Doctor, what are the next steps? What therapy will she need?"

The air sharpened. Van's father turned on her. "Don't you start, Leslie. She's not your mama."

Uncle David—tall, silent, oldest—stood behind his wife like a wall. He didn't speak. He didn't have to.

"She's my mother-in-law," Leslie said, chin lifted. "And David's mother."

"What she needs," the doctor tried again, "is rest. Limited visitors. Time."

"Rest?" Van's father barked a laugh that wasn't laughter. "You expect us to sit on our hands while she fades?"

The doctor pressed his lips thin, nodded once, and retreated —grateful for distance. In his wake, the family noise flared: Leslie's pointed whisper, David's stone-still quiet, an aunt's breathless prayer.

Van pressed his back to the cool wall. Most of the words slid off him. One sound stuck, carrying through the glass: a soft, metronomic tone—beep...beep...beep. The only rhythm in the building that mattered.

In the waiting room, grief became theater. Van's father collapsed into a plastic chair, elbows to knees, face in his hands, the sobs that wracked him tearing the quiet in jagged strips. "She's my mama," he gasped. "She don't deserve this."

Leslie watched, eyes glittering with heat. "We all love her. We need the right decisions."

"Decisions?" his father snapped, lifting a streaked face. "You think this is paperwork?" His voice cracked back into a cry. The cousins stared at the floor. An aunt tried a hymn and lost her place on the second line.

The family's voices climbed and tangled. Van slid down the far wall until tile met his spine. Beyond the fluorescent hum and vending machine rattle, that steady pulse threaded the noise—faint, high, alive. Beep. Beep. Beep. He shut his eyes and held onto it like a rope in water.

When no one watched, he slipped through the ICU door. Antiseptic and metal threaded the air. Machines blinked steady constellations around the bed. His grandmother seemed smaller, swallowed by sheets, skin pale against the white. The slackness of her face hurt to look at, and still the room felt more hers than anywhere else in the hospital.

He pulled a chair close and took her hand. The skin was thinner than tissue, cool against his palm. Memory rushed in without asking: Sunday mornings when he'd sit pressed against her side, his arm under hers, tracing the soft map of wrinkles while the preacher thundered and her thumb tapped time on the hymnal. He pressed her hand to his forehead. "Grandma," he whispered, "it's me. I'm here."

The monitor answered with the same small courage: beep.

"They're all out there making a mess," he said, voice shaking and quiet, "but I don't care about any of that. I just need you." He thought he felt the faintest twitch in her fingers, and the hope that flared hurt worse than anything. He waited. Her eyelids fluttered once and stilled.

"Please don't go," he breathed. The room offered nothing back but the hum of machines and that thin, stubborn heartbeat of sound.

A week later she came home—not healed, not whole, but moved to hospice. The floral sofa he used to sink into when she read stories had been pushed against the wall to make space for the hospital bed. The house smelled like antiseptic wipes and lotion instead of cornbread and furniture polish.

Aides learned the floorboards quickly, moving with practiced care. One was young and soft-voiced, a man whose hands couldn't be rattled. It was enough to set Van's father off. He stood in the doorway, arms crossed. "A man? Taking care of her like that?"

"It's my job," the aide said, gentler than the room deserved. "I treat all my patients with dignity."

"That ain't decent," Van's father spat. "She don't need some stranger—some man—handling her."

"Medical care," Leslie cut in. "Stop making a spectacle."

But spectacle was the only language the house spoke. The living room didn't feel like his grandmother's anymore. It felt like a stage. Van stayed small in a corner of it and listened for the one sound that kept telling the truth.

Beep. Beep. Beep.

CHAPTER 13
THE QUIET THAT KNOWS YOUR NAME

The young hospice nurse returned in faded blue scrubs. He adjusted the quilt with gentle fingers, checked the line of the oxygen tubing, and when he leaned forward, a pin on his badge caught the lamplight—a small gold enamel rainbow.

"What's that supposed to mean?" Van's father barked, pointing as if the pin were a threat.

The nurse glanced down and back up, voice even. "It's a pin."

"A rainbow pin," his father pressed. "Does that mean you're —" He let the word rot in the air.

Van felt the floor shift under him.

"I'm here to care for your mother," the nurse said, calm as a steady hand. "That's what matters."

"That ain't an answer," his father huffed.

"Sometimes a pin is just a pin," the nurse said, and gently lifted a pillow, his touch sure, unflinching. The gold glinted once more, not loud—just there.

After he left, the house seemed louder for his absence. Van

held that quiet look, the way a person could occupy a room without apology, and felt the edges of himself ache.

His mother decided they needed air. "We'll go home for a few hours," she said, kneading purpose into each word. "I'll cook something to take back."

At their house, she attacked the kitchen like a battle she knew how to win, flour dusting the counter, biscuit cutter flashing, foil pans rattling. Van drifted down the hall to his room. The silence pressed like a palm to his chest. The phone rang.

"Why didn't you tell me?" Dana demanded the second he picked up. "I had to hear from my mama that your grandma's in hospice."

"I didn't want to—"

"You think you're a bother to me?" A car door slammed beneath her voice. "Fifteen minutes."

She was in the driveway in ten, ponytail crooked, a half-smashed bag of chips under her arm. "You look like hell," she announced, dropping onto the porch step beside him. She thrust the bag into his lap. "Eat."

Salt hit his tongue like electricity. The cicadas were a wall of sound in the trees, the smell of baking biscuits drifting from the kitchen like a memory.

"None of the guys called," he said finally. "Not one."

Dana snorted. "Those boys wouldn't notice a train through their living room. They're too busy pretending the world is fine. That's why you've got me."

He stared at his hands. "Do you ever feel like God messed you up? Like everyone else came out right, and I came out wrong?" The words shook. "I pray and nothing changes. Maybe I'm defective."

Dana turned, all the fire in her eyes settling into a steady light. "People are messed up," she said. "Not God. And you're not defective. You feel too much—more than they're brave enough to. That's not broken. That's real."

He swallowed, heat stinging his eyes. "My dad's on me, the church is watching, and I don't even know what I am half the time."

She jabbed his shoulder. "Don't you dare call yourself a mistake. Your grandma loves you because you're you. I do, too. Now eat the chips and cry if you need to. I'm not going anywhere."

He laughed once, shaky, and did both.

Sunday morning, his father tied the darkest tie he owned. The sanctuary smelled like hymnals and floor polish. Heads turned, whispers rippled, sympathy and curiosity braided together. Van felt the eyes like a weight.

"Go up when they ask for prayers," his father breathed, the words sharp enough to cut. "Stand straight. Let them know you're her grandson."

When Pastor Rich called for requests, his father's hand flew up. "My mother!" he cried. "Struck down but not defeated. I need every saint in this room on their knees."

And then Van was shoved into the aisle. The floorboards creaked under his shoes. He found his way to the front and forced words through a throat that had decided to close. "Please pray for my grandma. She... she needs healing." His voice trembled. Amens murmured. A hand pressed heavy to his shoulder.

He made it back to the pew and felt his pulse in his teeth. His father leaned in, satisfied. "That's it. That's how they'll know we're faithful."

The sermon unfurled like cloth over a table that had already been set. Van stared at the hymnboard and heard Dana in his head: You're not broken. You're the sane one.

That night, when the house finally surrendered to a lull— mother asleep, father snoring in his chair—Van stepped onto the back porch. The heat had softened, crickets trading the day's clamor for an older song. Fireflies stitched light in and out of the hedges.

He thought of the nurse. The small pin. The steady voice: I'm here to care for your mother. That's what matters.

"God," Van said to the dark, "if You made me wrong, why does remembering him feel more right than anything else?" The words came like something unsplinters. "I don't understand You. I don't understand how I'm supposed to be ashamed of what looks like peace on somebody else."

He waited for an answer and got the night. It wasn't empty. It wasn't enough. He drew his knees to his chest and sat very still while the yard breathed around him, the one clear picture in his mind a tiny arc of rainbow enamel catching the lamp and refusing to apologize.

CHAPTER 14
THE UNEXPECTED ANCHOR

By late afternoon the next day, the nurse stood at the foot of the bed, voice quiet but firm. "Her breathing has weakened. Her body is beginning to shut down. These next days... you'll want to be present with her."

The words struck the room like a match in dry grass. Van's father folded into himself and then exploded, sobs tearing free. "No—God, no! Mama, don't you leave me! Don't you leave your baby boy!" He clutched the bedrail and rocked it like a cradle. Leslie pressed a dramatic hand to her chest and leaned into David's stillness. Prayers rose like steam. An aunt moaned. Someone said hallelujah like it could make the clock run backward.

From the doorway, a voice sliced through the noise. "She can't rest with all that hollerin'."

Aunt Shelia stepped in with a stack of Tupperware and a look that brooked no foolishness. She thunked the containers onto the dining table and rolled up her sleeves. "I brought food," she said. "Figured no one remembered you still gotta eat to live."

"You don't know what it's like to lose your mama!" Van's father shot back, red-eyed, chest heaving.

"Maybe not," Shelia said, soft as a steel bar. "But I know she deserves peace, not a circus. You wanna cry, cry. But stop making it about you."

He deflated into a chair with a shuddering breath and settled for loud sniffles and pointed sighs. The room exhaled. Machines reclaimed the air. The oxygen hissed; the monitor kept its small witness. For the first time all week, quiet had a chance to stretch its legs.

The aides worked around it, lowering blinds, adjusting pillows, the economy of motion that comes from loving skill. The male nurse moved like tide, patient and precise. The gold pin flashed once when he reached across the quilt. Van's father saw it and his mouth twitched like it wanted a fight, but Shelia's presence across the room held him.

Van watched the care more than the chaos—the way a body could be tended like a sacred thing without any speeches to explain it. The storm of the house dulled at the edges. For a little while, breathing felt possible.

As evening slid its shoulder against the windows, Shelia caught Van's eye and tilted her head toward the porch. He followed her out. The air smelled faintly of honeysuckle; cicadas had taken over from the day shift. Shelia eased down the steps and produced two sodas from her bag like a magician.

"Better medicine than what's in there," she said, handing him one.

He cracked the tab and let the fizz burn a path down his throat.

"How you holding up?" she asked, and then, before he could lie, "Tell the truth."

"I want to sit with her," he said. "Everybody else wants to be seen loving her louder than the next person. If I don't join in, it feels like I don't love her enough. Like I'm wrong."

"Don't you ever mistake noise for love," Shelia said. "Your grandma knew you. Knew you didn't need to prove a thing."

He stared at the yard. "Do you ever think God gets it wrong? Like He makes people by mistake?"

Shelia tipped her head, took a long sip, set the can between her shoes. "No. I think people get Him wrong. On purpose sometimes."

"I keep praying," he said, voice fraying, "and I don't change. If He made me this way, then I'm the flaw no one wants to admit."

She let the quiet sit between them a moment, not heavy, just honest. "The only mistake here is somebody convincing you you're less than what you are," she said at last. "You hear me? You're not broken. You're you. And you're truer than half the performers in that room."

He wiped his face with the heel of his hand. "The church—"

"Is full of folks worried how they look in a pew," she said. "Your grandma didn't need you to perform. She needed your presence. That's what you've been giving her."

The cicadas swelled and eased. He took another drink and felt the first steady thing in days settle someplace under his ribs.

"Get used to me saying it," Shelia added, nudging his knee with the toe of her shoe. "You're not alone. Not while I'm breathing."

He believed her.

CHAPTER 15
THE WEIGHT OF VOICES

The prayer circle arrived with ceremony. The front door opened and Pastor Rich stepped in, Bible tucked under his arm, worry lining his face without cracking his composure. Just behind him came Coach Thomas—Colby's dad —jaw set in a Sunday kind of seriousness. Jeremiah trailed his father, hands shoved in his pockets, eyes on the floor until they lifted and found Van.

The room swelled for the audience. Van's father stood and made grief louder. "Pastor, the devil's been attacking my mama!" he cried, clutching the rail. "But we'll stand firm!"

"Amen," Coach Thomas rumbled.

Pastor Rich nodded to the gathered family. "Let us pray."

They pressed around the bed. The house became a chorus— hallelujahs braided to sobs, amens dropped like confetti. Van stayed near the sofa, anchored to the small rise and fall under the quilt. Jeremiah edged away from the circle until he leaned against the wall across from Van. When their eyes met, Jeremiah's mouth lifted—small, deliberate, not mocking. Across the room, Colby saw it, pushed his hands deeper into his pockets, and stared at the rug.

When the prayers crested and fell, Van didn't feel changed. He felt scraped thin.

"Here," Shelia said from the doorway, a plate stacked with cornbread, beans, and a slice of ham balanced in her palm. "Eat."

He hesitated.

"Now." She steered him to the kitchen and left him at the table. The house's noise muffled at the bend in the hall. The beans tasted like something that could keep a person alive.

"You've probably not eaten since breakfast," she said, leaning on the counter.

"I wasn't hungry."

"You mean no one noticed," she said, not unkindly.

The living room surged again—Pastor Rich's voice lifting, Coach Thomas's low yes, Lord in the right places, Van's father restarting the sermon of his sorrow for anyone who had missed the earlier performance. Shelia rolled her eyes skyward. "You'd think they were auditioning."

Van almost laughed. Almost. He finished the cornbread, and the ground under him steadied another inch.

When the amen drifted down the hall and the bodies shifted toward the porch, Van slipped back into the living room. The oxygen hissed; the monitor kept time. The bed was an island in the clearing. He moved to the entertainment center and crouched at the bottom shelf, fingertips tracing the familiar edges of old record sleeves until he found what he was looking for—ELVIS in rubbed-off gold.

He slid the vinyl out with a care he used for almost nothing else, set it on the turntable, and lowered the needle. The machine crackled—warm, imperfect—and then music found the air like a voice you didn't know you needed to hear.

He pulled the chair to the bed and took her hand. "This

one's for you," he whispered, and began to sing with the record, low and ragged:

"Are you lonesome tonight..."

The melody wore its years like a quilt. He leaned close, forehead almost to hers, and let his throat ache on each line. For a heartbeat he felt her fingers tell on themselves, the tiniest answering press against his palm, and he broke and kept going anyway.

When the song clicked to silence, he kissed her knuckles and rested them against his cheek. "I love you, Grandma," he said into the quiet that knew his name. "I won't stop."

Voices drifted through the open windows—Pastor Rich's baritone floating with the aunts' and uncles' amens, Coach Thomas adding his low reply, Van's father retelling the nurse's warning yet again for the porch. For the first time all day, the living room was empty.

The screen door creaked. Jeremiah stepped onto the porch and then reappeared at the threshold, as if deciding. He slipped inside and nodded toward the door with a tilt of his head. Van followed him out.

Night wrapped the porch in hum and heat. Shelia had taken the swing and then, seeing them, vacated it with a soda and a look that said I see what I see. She wandered into the yard.

"You holding up?" Jeremiah asked, voice pitched small.

"Better than they think I am," Van said, surprised at how true it sounded.

Jeremiah's gaze flicked to the window where the lamp gilded the bedrail. "You're starting to look like you don't care what they think," he said—all fear and admiration in one breath. "I don't know how to do that."

"I'm just tired," Van said. "Of pretending. Of the show."

Jeremiah studied the boards under his shoes. "Me too," he said, and then, quieter, "in more ways than one."

"I'm not asking you to be ready," Van said. The words surprised him by being steady. "Just to be real."

Jeremiah looked up at that. A slow smile found the corner of his mouth. "That's what scares me about you."

The screen door groaned. "Boys," Pastor Rich called, not unkindly, "we're going to lay hands and sing one more."

"I should go back in," Jeremiah said. "Before my dad notices."

"Yeah." Van wasn't sure what either of them had just promised, only that something had been named without either of them saying it out loud.

"Can I... can I see you again?" Jeremiah asked. "Just... talk."

"Anytime," Van said.

Jeremiah slipped back inside. Van stood on the porch until the cicadas' rhythm braided itself into that other rhythm that had followed him all week—the little sound that refused to quit. He stepped to the window and watched his grandmother breathe.

Beep. Beep. Beep.

It wasn't triumph. It wasn't despair. It was the small, stubborn truth that held when everything else was noise. And for the first time since the stroke, he knew what to call the feeling under his ribs.

Not broken.

Held.

"Some silences are holy; some are just heavy. Learn the difference."

———GRANDMA

CHAPTER 16
THE FINAL CURTAIN

The house didn't sound like itself anymore. Gone were the layered noises of a family in motion—the squeak of the front door under a parade of casserole dishes, aunts whispering in corners, chairs scraping over linoleum. What remained was the hiss of the oxygen concentrator and the steady tick of the mantle clock, two stubborn metronomes keeping time no one wanted.

Van sat close, knees nearly touching the bedrail, his grandmother's hand resting in his palm—paper-thin, blue-veined, familiar. He rubbed his thumb slowly over her knuckles the way she'd soothed him when he was small, back when worry could be rocked to sleep at her kitchen table.

"I'm right here, Grandma," he whispered, leaning in so the words belonged to her alone. "I'm not going anywhere."

Her chest rose and fell, shallow and uneven beneath the quilt.

The nurse eased in, movements unhurried, voice the same soft level he always kept. He adjusted the pillows, checked the line of oxygen, glanced at the monitor that had stopped blinking anything except a stubborn green dot. "She's comfortable," he said, meeting Van's eyes, the quiet of his face a mercy. Then he slipped out and let the door hush shut behind him.

Silence grew heavier once he was gone.

"It's okay," Van breathed, his forehead resting against the back of her hand. "If you're tired... you can rest. I'll be fine."

The clock ticked. The oxygen hissed.

She drew one breath. Then another—slower, thinner.

And then she didn't.

Stillness arrived all at once, absolute.

He held her hand tighter and waited for the quilt to lift again, even a little. When it didn't, the word scraped out of him raw. "No..."

He pressed his face to her fingers, the heat of his tears soaked into her cool skin. "Please... not yet."

The clock kept its indifferent count. The machine hummed on, a sound with nothing left to do.

Van stayed like that, grief muffled against her palm, until the walls shook with his father's wail.

"Mama! My mama!" His father stumbled to the bed, voice tearing itself ragged. He clutched at the quilt like he could anchor her back with his hands. The door flew wide; relatives filled the frame, then the room—choked sobs, prayers, the scrape of chairs, everyone staking their piece of sorrow.

Aunt Leslie pressed both palms to her chest and rocked on her heels. "Oh Lord, oh Lord," she moaned, leaning into Uncle David's square silence. David's jaw locked so tight it looked carved; his eyes shone but didn't spill. The cousins arranged themselves in little clumps—one weeping into the same tissue every time someone looked her way, another crossing his arms with eyes damp but watchful, as if restraint might earn him credit.

It was grief. It was also a performance.

Emmalee found Van's side and clung, her small sobs high

and sharp. He wrapped an arm around her and let her shake against him. "I've got you," he whispered, even though he didn't feel like he had anything at all.

The hospice staff edged back in, gentle logic cutting a path through the noise. "We need to prepare her now," one aide said. The room drew a breath and made space.

The white sheet whispered as they smoothed it over his grandmother's face. That soft brush of fabric was louder than every cry. The men from the funeral home arrived in black—faces practiced, steps precise—and lifted her carefully. Quilt and sheet, the shape of a life carried through her living room to a silent car at the curb.

Van's knees went weak.

Arms wrapped around him—steady, unsentimental, unshakable. "I got you, baby," Aunt Shelia murmured at his ear. "Don't hold back."

The dam gave. He let it all tear loose—fear, love, weight—and Shelia held the back of his head and gave him a little patch of privacy in a room full of watchers.

It didn't last. "Chairs!" Leslie called over the quiet. "We'll need more chairs before Pastor Rich gets here. And the good tablecloths—not the faded ones."

"Van," his father barked, the command breaking mid-sylla-ble, "do as your aunt says. Help get this house ready."

He eased Emmalee onto the sofa and pressed a cousin's hand to her shoulder. Then the evening blurred into errands. He set out folded chairs in two tight rows, hauled in foil-covered dishes, shook hands with people he was told were kin. "This is your uncle's cousin's boy," his father said once, presenting a stranger. "Show respect."

"Thank you for being here," Van answered, the phrase becoming its own numb muscle in his mouth.

When the house had been reset for grief, the hospital bed

stood stripped bare. The quilt his grandmother loved lay folded on a chair. Out here, sorrow had a script; in there, it had felt like the truth.

The sanctuary smelled of lilies and beeswax. The casket gleamed under the lights, open and impossibly neat—hair curled, hands folded over her Bible, her smallness sharpened by all that care. Van sat front row, shouldered in between Emmalee and his father's quaking bulk, and didn't look away.

"Amazing Grace" rose behind him, voices layered soft, then full. Later, a man from the choir loft poured out "It Is Well." The deep notes rattled the pews; his father's sobs rode the top of it, loud and shaking. Van's tears slid quiet and steady. The hymns carved for him what his own voice couldn't.

When Pastor Rich asked the congregation to bow their heads, Van did not. His gaze moved heavy and slow across the room. A few pews back, Jeremiah's eyes were open too. They found each other and held. Jeremiah didn't look away.

"Amen," Pastor Rich said at last. Bodies rustled; Van snapped his eyes forward. The deacons called the pallbearers. His name had been read earlier and felt like a stone in his stomach. Now it dropped.

He rose on legs that didn't believe in themselves and took the brass handle with his cousins. The weight surprised him with how sure it was. The organ swelled. They walked.

At the graveside, the sun pressed its hand on everything. Red clay yawned open. Van's palms slipped slick as they set the casket on the rails. Pastor Rich prayed about rest and reunion; Scripture fluttered over the heat.

Van heard none of it. His chest seized and the world titled.

Shelia reached and paused, eyes flicking past him. Jeremiah stood just outside the family arc, jaw tight, eyes fixed. She stepped back—an unspoken invitation.

Jeremiah crossed the space without hesitating and slid an

arm around Van's shoulders, the other hand catching his forearm like an anchor. "It's okay," he said, voice low and certain. "I've got you."

Van turned into him and let himself break. It wasn't the polite tears of the pew or the private sobs in a quiet room—it was everything, out loud. Jeremiah didn't shush him or straighten him. He just stood and held.

Across the circle, Colby looked up. His jaw tensed; his hands stayed wedged in his pockets. Something sharp flashed over his face—longing, regret—before he smoothed it into a joke for the boy beside him. It didn't quite stick.

Van's fists closed in the fabric of Jeremiah's jacket. He felt the steady rise of Jeremiah's chest beneath his cheek and, for the first time all week, something inside cracked open all the way with someone there to see.

When he finally leaned back, Jeremiah's hand stayed at the nape of his neck. Their eyes met—unashamed, new—and the air shifted, heavy with more than grief.

Shovels bit clay. Red earth thudded against the lid. Voices tried to outsing the sound. From just behind, a whisper bled forward: "Did you see how close he was holding him?" Another replied, certain: "Not like a friend." A man muttered, "Not here."

Heat climbed the back of Van's neck. Shelia turned, and the whispers died like candles pinched out. She didn't say a word.

The fellowship hall sagged under casseroles and fried chicken, the clang of serving spoons against Pyrex passing for conversation. Condolences came out like vocabulary words. Van slid toward the wood-paneled wall and wished he could pass through it.

"Move, people!" Dana barreled in, balancing a plate and a cup of tea, her ponytail defiant. She shoved the plate into his hands. "Eat before you fall over."

"I'm not—"

"Don't care." She leaned closer, voice for him alone. "I saw the way they looked at you. Let them choke on their own casseroles. You hear me? You don't owe them explanation for needing someone."

His laugh was small and real. The food tasted like salt and mercy.

Around them the roles held: Coach Thomas booming about soccer schedules, Seth posted on a wall with his arms crossed and his eyes too interested, Colby laughing too loudly then falling silent when he forgot. Pastor Rich reappeared near the buffet, hand resting on Jeremiah's shoulder like a claim.

"Van, honey," Ms. Denise sang as she swept past, "could you run more napkins to the drink table?" Her smile was sweet and supervisory. "The menfolk get clumsy with their sweet tea."

"Always leaning on Van to do the work," Seth murmured, just loud enough.

"Van, son, good to see you keepin' busy," Coach Thomas called from across the room. "Your daddy's raised you right— always serving."

"Thank you, sir," Van managed, and the words scraped on the way out.

Jeremiah drifted back, voice lowered to a thread. "I know I can't be like you," he said. "I can't be that brave. Not yet. Maybe not ever. But I need you to know I see you. I see all of it. And I—"

"Jeremiah." Pastor Rich's hand settled heavier on his son's shoulder. "Help your mother with the serving spoons. Don't sit idle while the ladies do the work."

Jeremiah's mouth closed on the rest. He looked at Van, the unsaid burning between them. "Later," he whispered.

The word landed and stayed.

He disappeared into the kitchen bustle, swallowed by the rhythm of the hall. Colby's glance cut across to Van and away again. Seth watched like a man waiting for a storm. The pastor moved on to the next cluster of hands to shake and backs to clap.

Everyone in their place. Everyone in character. Van stood with a stack of napkins in one hand and a plate in the other, held up by two things that weren't casseroles—an arm around him at the grave, a friend planting her feet in front of him now.

"Later," echoed once more in his chest.

But not tonight.

CHAPTER 17

THE BURDEN OF INDEPENDENCE

The DMV smelled like bleach wiped over yesterday's coffee. Plastic chairs ran in obedient rows beneath humming lights; somewhere a printer clicked and stalled and clicked again, like even the machines were exhausted. Van sat with his knee bouncing, palms damp on a folded sheet that suddenly felt more like a verdict than a test score.

His mother smoothed the corner of her skirt for the tenth time. "Don't slouch, Van. You're seventeen now, not a little boy."

He straightened. The clock on the far wall refused to budge. When they finally called his name, the world telescoped— mirrors, signals, a tidy parallel park he'd practiced behind the Piggly Wiggly, the examiner's pen making short, decisive checks. "Congratulations," she said, sliding the signed form toward him.

It should have been air in his lungs. Freedom, in paper form.

In the car, doors shut, seat belts clicking, his mother's expression shifted. "Well. That's done. Now comes the responsibility."

"I passed, Mom. Can you just... be happy for me for one second?"

"I am happy." Her voice thinned. "But a license means more work for us. You'll take Emmalee every morning, pick her up every afternoon. No excuses. And you'll get a job—gas doesn't pay for itself. Your daddy won't bankroll joyrides."

"I haven't even driven alone yet."

"Don't start with that tone." She kept her eyes on the road, knuckles white on the wheel. "We can take this away the second you give us a reason. One bad grade, one late curfew—gone. Understand?"

The paper in his hands grew heavier. A rite of passage already ringed with warning tape. "Yes, ma'am."

She sighed, softer but still edged. "You're just growing up so fast. It's hard on us too."

He pressed his forehead to the glass and watched the world go by in slices.

They turned onto their street, the house coming into view, and that's when he saw it—parked crooked on the gravel, paint sun-faded to a dark green that turned gray in shade. A BMW sedan, or what time had left of one. The chrome trim pitted, the leather cracked, the hood a map of hairline scratches. The emblem on the grille was bleached but undeniable: BMW.

His mother cut the engine. "Surprise," she said, as if the word had been assigned to her.

Heat rolled up from the driveway. Van slid a hand over the hood; the metal felt rough, more truth than shine. This was his car. It also wasn't, not really.

He gripped the keys and settled into the driver's seat. "New Car Scent" fogged the air, valiantly failing to win against old leather and hot vinyl. The ignition coughed twice, then caught. For the first time ever, no one claimed the passenger seat. The emptiness felt like possibility.

Gravel popped under the tires as he backed out, the dash rattling in a way that said be gentle. He pointed the nose toward church like muscle memory. In the lot, trucks and sedans lined the spaces closest to the door. He tucked the BMW farther out and cut the engine. Cicadas filled the humid dark.

"Van?" Travis and Seth drifted across the asphalt, Colby just behind them, laughter trailing like a kite tail.

"Look at you," Travis said, clapping Van's shoulder. "Rolling up in style."

"It's twenty years old," Van muttered.

"Still a Beemer." Seth cocked his head, then barked a laugh. "What's that?"

Van squinted at the bumper, and his stomach dropped. The front novelty plate—bold block letters—gleamed under the floodlight: THANKS DAD!

His ears went hot.

"Bet your dad made you kiss his shoes for that one," Travis snorted.

Van shouldered past them. Cool air met him in the vestibule, but embarrassment stuck like humidity. He'd barely reached the front pew when his father's voice caught him.

"Son." Suit pressed, chin lifted, eyes bright with a public kind of pride. "You park up front where your friends could see? Make sure they knew what your mama and I bought you?"

"They saw it."

"That's right." His father's smile sharpened. "A BMW. Not some rusty Ford like the rest of them." A clap between the shoulder blades, hard enough to sting. "You remember to tell folks that. Not everybody's as blessed as you."

The choir warmed up. Van slipped into a pew and traced the frayed edge of a hymnal. Independence had arrived with a plate that shouted who deserved thanks.

When the benediction faded and the piano sighed its last,

the aisles swelled with small talk. At the end of their row, his mother's hug came with a whisper: "Straight home, Van. No stopping." His father boomed loud enough for heads to turn: "Get that parking pass first thing tomorrow. Don't want my boy's BMW towed on day one."

Outside, the lot hummed. Engines revved. Kids split like water around bumpers and knees. Van angled toward the far spaces, toward his car—where a figure leaned against the hood, swallowed by shadow. He jangled his keys; the figure shifted into the spill of the church sign's light.

Jeremiah.

Tie loosened, hands in pockets, eyes shadowed but sure. "You survived," he said.

"Barely." Van's keys trembled in his hand.

Noise eddied around them—Colby's laugh near the trucks, Coach Thomas's voice booming goodnights, Seth calling across rows. Jeremiah's voice dipped. "I meant what I said at the hall. You're stronger than they think. Stronger than me."

"It doesn't feel like it."

"That's because they don't let you feel it." His glance tipped toward the glass doors, then back. He leaned just close enough for the word to reach without traveling. "Later. I promise."

Headlights washed the asphalt—his parents creeping past. His father leaned out the window: "Straight home! No fooling around!"

Van lifted a hand. By the time he turned back, Jeremiah had melted into the crowd. "Drive safe," he said, then was gone.

Van slid behind the wheel and gripped the cracked leather. His first drive alone, and he could feel every eye that wasn't even looking. The engine complained, then settled. He stayed put, just long enough to let the word lodge where he could feel it: Later.

Morning bled through blinds. The keys on his dresser

caught the light like a dare. At breakfast his mother laid out rules between bites of toast—straight to school, no detours, pick up Emmalee, applications tonight. His father added curfew, eyes on his plate.

The drive to school was mostly quiet—Emmalee humming, a teacher's name, a story about a lopsided diorama. She hopped out at the middle school with a wave and hurry up, you're blocking, and then the car felt too big for one person and too small for all the thoughts inside it.

At the high school curb, Dana yanked the passenger door open before he'd fully stopped. "Well, well," she said, tossing her bag into the back. "Mr. Big Shot." Her gaze slid to the front bumper and she snorted. "Oh no. Tell me that doesn't say what I think it says."

"Don't."

She leaned back, grinning. "It's campy. I love it. Half this lot would trade a kidney for an engine that turns over. Let them perform rage; we've got places to be." She tapped the dash. "And by 'places' I mean Sonic after school, me in your passenger seat, and us pretending the world is less terrible than it is."

He laughed, tension easing. It came back as he slid into a spot and killed the engine—curfew, gas, grades, the weight of the family name hitching a ride on his rearview mirror.

The last bell spilled everyone into heat and exhaust. Dana claimed her seat like she'd paid for it. They snagged Emmalee from the middle school just as she burst through the doors, braid unraveling, narration unspooling. At home, Em bailed with a wave and a door slam. For a heartbeat the house framed his mother in the screen door, cataloging, measuring. Dana lifted a hand.

"So," she said, gum snapping as they idled. "What's the deal with Jeremiah?"

"What?"

"Don't play dumb." Her smile softened into something that wasn't a smile at all. "Are you gay, Van?"

The word hit hard and clean. His hands tightened on the wheel. Air thickened. He opened his mouth. Closed it. The engine ticked quietly as it cooled.

Dana didn't move, didn't blink. "Yeah," she said, almost tender. "You do know."

He turned the key again because doing something felt safer than answering. "Applications," he muttered. "I need to fill out applications."

"Fine," she said, as if she hadn't just picked up his heart, checked its pulse, and handed it back. "But you're eating at my house. Meatloaf. And you'll be home by that ridiculous curfew or your parents will call in a helicopter."

He stuck his head inside long enough to tell his mother where he'd be; she reminded him how many places his father expected to hear he'd applied. Back in the car Dana buckled in and clapped. "To capitalism! And uncomfortable truths."

They did the rounds. At the grocery, Mr. Jenkins's toupee leaned left while Van filled out a form on a sticky counter as Dana scolded bruised peaches like they'd sinned. At the bowling alley, a kid with a volcano of acne warned him in a whisper: don't get stuck on shoes; the smell never leaves. At the hardware store, a woman with a vest full of pins gave them a twenty-minute update on her cat's kidney situation. Dana patted her arm like they were family. "Poor Mittens," she said gravely.

By the time the scent of meatloaf pulled them into Dana's driveway, the sun had dropped low. Dinner was loud with good questions and gentle steering; whenever her mother asked too much about the car, Dana set the conversation in a new lane. Later, in Dana's room with the door cleverly angled to satisfy house rules, Van picked at a thread on the quilt while Dana sank into her beanbag.

"So," she said, easy as a song she knew by heart. "Back to Jeremiah."

"Dana..."

"You don't have to dance." Her voice wasn't sharp now. It was steady. "Are you gay?"

Silence stretched, then thinned. The box fan rattled. Somewhere down the hall, a cabinet shut. Van felt the word in his mouth before he heard it.

"I—" His throat scraped. "I don't know. I mean... maybe. Probably." He shut his eyes. "Yes."

There it was in the room, unhidden: I'm gay.

He braced for something to crack—the ceiling, his chest, the ground beneath the house. Instead, the only thing that broke was the hold fear had on his lungs.

Dana's grin came fierce and bright. "About damn time."

The laugh that jumped out of him turned into a sob halfway. Relief rushed through like air after being held under. Tears came hot and bewildering and not the same as grief. She launched off the beanbag and hugged him so hard he wheezed.

"You're my best friend," she said into his shoulder. "If anybody messes with you, they'll find out I have excellent teeth."

He laughed again, wetter this time. "I was so scared."

"I know." She leaned back to see his face. "You don't have to be scared with me. We keep it close, on your terms. You say who, when, how. Until then? You've got me."

He nodded, everything in him shaking and settling at once. The fear hadn't evaporated, but something louder had taken its place. He said it again, softer, more certain.

"I'm gay."

It didn't crush him. It fit.

That night, alone behind the wheel with the windows cracked and cicadas pouring their endless song, he took the long way home. He drove past the dark shape of the church where a father's hand rested heavy on a son's shoulder, past the cemetery fence where red clay had settled, past the house where the mantle clock kept counting in a newly quiet room. He didn't stop. He didn't speed.

At a four-way where no one came, he let the car idle and rested his forehead on the heel of his hand. In the rearview, the novelty plate winked in the glow of the brake lights—THANKS DAD!—loud as a billboard. Van snorted, half laugh, half breath.

"Later," he whispered into the dashboard, into the dark, into the promise still warm on his skin.

Then he put the car in gear and went home before curfew, the word riding shotgun all the way.

"A good diner teaches two religions: refill and respect."

———GRANDMA

CHAPTER 18
THE DINER SHIFT

The weeks after Van's first solo drive blurred into a loop of applications and interrogations. Every night ended the same: his father's voice at the table, sharp with inventory.

"Where'd you apply?"

"Was it respectable?"

"Don't waste time on dead-end jobs."

His mother followed with soft-voiced lists that cut just as deep. "Keep your grades up, Van. Emmalee still needs rides. Driving isn't freedom—it's responsibility."

He filled out form after form under the kitchen light while the THANKS DAD plate on the BMW winked at him through the window like a dare. Dana came along to most places, filling the silence whenever managers' questions made his throat go dry.

"You're already hired as my paid chauffeur-slash-therapist," she told him, bumping his shoulder outside the hardware store. "Now let's trick someone else into paying you, too."

It clicked at Magnolia Grill.

The building squatted beside the highway with peeling paint and a neon sign that buzzed even when it slept. The room smelled like coffee that had been warm all day and bacon that had never quite left. Marlene slid an application across the counter, looked him over once, and said, "You've got a steady look about you. We could use steady."

Dana elbowed him, grinning. "Told you."

A week later, he stood in the cramped employee bathroom, tugging a gray t-shirt with MAGNOLIA GRILL across the chest. The visor pinched his forehead; the apron strings bit a hard knot at his back. The mirror's crack ran through his reflection like a fault line. He looked older than he felt.

"Bless my soul," Dana drawled from the hostess stand when he stepped out. "Donovan Shelton, professional hash-slinger."

"You look ridiculous, too."

She threw a hand to her heart. "Excuse you. This is hostess chic. I'm the face of the establishment. You're just the legs."

From behind the grill, Frank lifted his spatula like a gavel. "Apron makes the man."

Marlene breezed past with a coffee pot. "Frank's never said that in his life." She tipped the pot toward Van's empty mug. "First week's rough. But you've got steady in you. That matters more than speed."

He didn't have words for the relief that line delivered. He nodded, wiped a clean counter anyway, and listened to the room.

The Grill was more a marriage than a business, and you could see it in the owners' orbit. Frank was square-shouldered, cap sweat-stained, working the grill like it extended from his wrist: flip the burger, sip the coffee, crack the joke. Marlene was all quick lines and quicker eyes, the coffee pot an extra limb, her voice efficient enough to cut through nonsense without raising an octave.

"You're a thinker," she said later, brushing past with a stack of plates.

"I guess."

Frank called from the grill. "Thinking's fine. Food don't wait on philosophers."

Marlene rolled her eyes; Van caught the smile tugging at her mouth. Their bickering wasn't sharp; it was choreography that had taken decades to learn. At home, everything felt like a performance for the audience in their heads. Here, people simply were.

"Religion's fine," Marlene added in a quiet spell, topping off old Mr. Garner's mug. "But when it turns into a contest of who sings the loudest or cries the hardest, that's theater. Exhausting."

"Best prayer I ever said was fishing," Frank said. "Didn't even say it out loud."

The regulars cast themselves without prompting. Farmers filled Booth Three, denim faded where it met truck seats. Retired mill hands claimed the counter stools like deeds. The perfume-heavy church ladies nested in the corner booth, lipstick rings on cups like little red halos.

Most were easy once he learned the cues. Coffee refilled before they looked up. Extra napkins when the chicken fried steak marched out. Nod along when two men argued over which tractor brand God favored.

Some were... extra.

Mrs. Callahan slapped her Bible on the Formica like it needed to be saved. "The Lord gave you good hair," she announced, squinting at his visor. "Shame covering it."

"Sweet tea?" Van asked.

"Half-sweet. Too much sugar is of the devil. Just like dancing."

"Whew," Dana called from the stand. "Thank you're not on Dancing with the Stars, Mrs. Callahan. We'd all be doomed."

Giggles from the next booth. Mrs. Callahan sniffed like she could excommunicate with her nose.

A gruff farmer jabbed a finger at Van's order pad. "Boy, don't let this job keep you from Wednesday night service. Lord don't take excuses."

"Pretty sure the Lord don't mind biscuits," Frank answered without looking up. "Long as they're fluffy."

Dana mouthed fluffy biscuits until Van nearly dropped a plate.

Even the church ladies had notes. "We saw your daddy Sunday," one cooed. "Fine Christian man. You best keep up, young Shelton."

"Yes, ma'am," he said, stomach tightening.

But the room corrected itself. Dana bent lamentably off-key into a Christmas carol while polishing menus. Marlene slid Van a clandestine slice of pie. Frank barked, "Hot hands!" with a grin big enough to lend.

He was learning to move in it. He was learning to breathe.

The dinner rush hit in waves: families first, then the regulars easing back in, and finally the late crowd—farmhands and truckers carrying dust and diesel through the door. The bell jingled, and the room changed one evening. Laughter arrived early, loud and thin.

Four young men walked in, boots loud on linoleum. Worn denim, grease-stained caps, shoulders built by work. One of them stalled Van mid-step—a little taller, the edges of his hair bleached by sun, jawline too sharp for the room. His flannel sleeves were rolled; his eyes—stormy gray—moved across the diner and landed on Van.

Air snagged in Van's chest. He was used to noticing and pretending not to. This noticing refused to be packed away.

"Order up!" Frank barked. Plates clattered; Van remembered to breathe.

He carried waters to their table.

"Well, what do we have?" one slouched, grinning at the visor. "A real professional."

"Sweet tea," said another, "unless that pot's got something stronger."

"Coke," a third added. "Bring it with a smile. Sweeten it up."

The tall one didn't laugh. He just watched, mouth tilted, like Van was an answer he'd expected to be wrong.

Van wrote quickly. Don't take the bait. Do the job.

As he turned to go, a voice slid after him. "Don't trip, sweetheart."

A chorus sniggered.

Dana was already moving, hips squared, ponytail a flag. "Hey," she snapped, planting herself at the end of their booth. "Harassing a server? That's low even for boots that muddy."

Marlene arrived with her coffee pot held like punctuation. "You boys want to eat here, you'll mind your manners. You don't like it, truck stop's a mile south. Our biscuits are better."

Silence flashed. Someone mumbled, "Teas are fine."

Dana shot Van a wink and returned to the stand like a gunslinger holstering. Marlene brushed Van's arm. "You're fine," she said for him alone. "Keep moving."

He did. For the first time in a long time, he didn't feel like he was standing alone.

CHAPTER 19
LINES IN THE GREASE

By the time Van returned with their drinks, the table had found its volume again.

"Look at him. Little visor. Apron tied tight."

"Bet he's never worked a field day in his life."

"Soft hands," someone smirked, leaning in. "You a sissy, boy? That why you're slingin' plates instead of hauling lumber like a man?"

Laughter cracked across the Formica.

The words were old in his body—cousins at cookouts, his father's tone when toughness came up, the tight smile he'd learned to wear when a joke kept going too long. For a second, seventeen felt like seven.

"Order up," Frank said—but this time his voice was closer.

He pushed through the swinging door with the spatula still in his hand and stopped at their table. He didn't raise his voice. He didn't have to.

"You boys done?"

"We're just having fun," one tried.

"Fun." Frank tapped the spatula against his palm, soft as a metronome. "I've run this grill longer than you've been shaving.

I've seen every kind of man sit at these tables. Farmers and truckers, mill hands and bankers. Saints, two of them. Sinners, plenty more. You know what makes a man?"

Chairs creaked. Even the fryer seemed to hush.

Frank pointed the spatula toward Van. "Showing up. Doing the work. Treating people right. That's it. You can't handle that, you ain't men. You're just noise."

He turned and vanished into the kitchen like he hadn't said a thing. The room exhaled.

Marlene's look pinned the booth to the vinyl. Dana's stance said try me twice. Van's hands shook once and then didn't. He set the teas down with a steady clink and walked away, spine finding a new line.

At home, the jokes slid past the adults and hit the quiet kid. Here, someone had stepped into the space and named what was true. Here, he counted.

The BMW rattled over gravel later, fryer oil and coffee stitched into his shirt. Emmalee commandeered the back seat with a breathless saga about blue pens and gym class tragedies.

"You rebel," Dana told her, feet on the dash, hair whipping in the open window. "Don't let the system cage your ink."

Em beamed. Van nodded when he was supposed to. At the curb, the porch light caught Emmalee's braid as she bounded inside. The door banged. It was only Dana now, humming tunelessly as she spun the radio knob through static into something old and dusty. She sang loud and wrong on purpose. He laughed once, and the knot in his chest let go another inch.

After a verse she went quiet. "Don't you listen to those jerks."

He drummed the steering wheel. The laughter still had a sting.

"You've got something they don't," she said. "Character. That terrifies people who need the world simple."

He glanced at her. Passing streetlights drew gold bands across her face. For the first time, the shape of what she said fit him.

Sunday tightened as November folded toward Christmas. The pastor's wife cornered him in the fellowship hall, voice sugared and sharp. "We're putting together the program, Van. Your daddy says you've got a fine voice. A reading? A solo? We need young men to set an example."

"Yes, ma'am," he said, because no was a word that didn't belong to Sheltons in church hallways.

His father stood nearby like a general. "Of course my boy will help. A Shelton stands out when duty calls."

The guys' knot re-formed in the lot the way storms re-form on hot days. "Hey, Van," Travis called, thumb aimed at the BMW. "Think you can give us a ride Wednesday? Save me gas."

"Yeah," Seth added. "We'll all pile in. Sharp to roll into the diner with a crew."

Colby hovered at the edge. His eyes flicked to Van, a flash of something unreadable, then away.

"Maybe," Van said.

Their ask wasn't him. It was the car—the convenience, the emblem. He felt it the way you feel humidity: not visible, but everywhere. The same boys who had turned their backs when he'd needed a shoulder angled toward him now because he had room in the backseat.

The grill's bell felt like oxygen that night. Frank teased him for over-stacking plates and then taught him the trick anyway. Marlene slipped him a wedge of pie big enough to be a kindness. Dana, off-key and delighted, mauled carols until Van bent behind the cooler and laughed where no one could see him.

Somewhere between a refill and a reorder, he realized exactly how split his life had become.

At church, he wore a last name like a uniform and did his

duty in a voice that didn't sound entirely like his own. At the diner, he wore polyester and a visor and somehow felt more himself than he ever had in starched sleeves.

He liked the boy wiping crumbs into his palm, steady on his feet, learning names and orders and the right time to pour. He liked the family that had opened around him without asking him to audition.

Near close, as he counted tips that smelled faintly of bacon grease, Marlene brushed past and said, "See? Steady."

Outside, the BMW's novelty plate winked in the glow of the sign. He snorted, shook his head, and slid behind the wheel. In the mirror, for a flicker, he saw the version of himself who'd walked into the DMV: tight, quiet, trying to take up less space than he occupied. Then he saw the one holding a tray that didn't shake.

Windows down, night air pouring in, he pulled onto the highway that ran between who he was expected to be and who he was becoming, and let the diner follow him home in the smell of coffee and fry oil and something like belonging.

CHAPTER 20
A HOLLOW CHRISTMAS

The boxes came down from the attic in a flurry one Saturday morning, his father barking orders from the living room while Van and Emmalee dragged dusty cardboard across the hallway. The smell of insulation clung to their clothes—dust and something old that always seemed to live in attic air.

Normally, this part had belonged to Grandma. She'd bring her own worn boxes from her house, each ornament wrapped in tissue paper softened by a dozen Christmases. Every piece had a story: the glass angel with one chipped wing she bought the first year she was married; the wooden train his grandfather carved before Van was born; the porcelain star she said reminded her of hope.

This year, those pieces were mixed into the Shelton boxes without a word.

Van froze when he unwrapped the chipped angel. The tissue still smelled faintly like Grandma's house—lavender and lemon polish—but now it had been folded into their jumble of tinsel and mismatched Santas.

Already? They'd already gone through her things?

Emmalee held up a porcelain reindeer, eyes wide. "This was Grandma's, wasn't it?"

Van nodded, his throat tight.

"Put that on the mantel, Em," their father called from the other room. "Higher up, where it looks nice."

Van turned toward him, the angel cupped in his hand. "Shouldn't we... ask before we put her things out like that?" His voice came careful, testing.

"They're family things," his father said, not looking up from the snarl of lights. "They belong to us now. Don't get sentimental."

"It just... feels fast."

That made his father pause. He straightened slowly, narrow-eyed. "You questioning me, boy? I said put it on the tree."

Van swallowed and lifted the angel carefully, tucking it into the branches where the lights would catch the chipped wing just right.

"That's fine," his father grunted. "But don't start acting like you know better than me. This is my house. I decide how things are done in it."

Van's fingers lingered against the needles. It wasn't a win, but it wasn't total surrender either. He had said the thing out loud. Maybe that counted.

He sank onto the couch for a minute while Emmalee placed the reindeer on the mantel exactly where she'd been told. She stepped back, face pinched.

She padded over and sat beside him, her whisper meant only for him. "It feels weird, doesn't it?"

"What does?"

"All this." She gestured at the tree and the boxes and the smell of dust and pine. "Grandma's things. Without Grandma. Like... they don't belong here."

He had expected her to miss the treats and the secrets and the songs. He hadn't expected her to notice this. "Yeah," he said softly. "It feels too soon."

She leaned her head against his arm. "I don't like it."

"Me neither, Em. Me neither."

Their father's voice boomed for more garland. Van pressed his hand to Em's back, stood, and went to fetch it.

A week before Christmas, they packed into the family car even though Van had offered—twice—to drive himself. "We show up as a family," his father said, no room for discussion. "Not scattered like strays."

They were headed to Uncle David and Aunt Leslie's for the "holiday planning dinner," another chance to assign casseroles and prayers, and to count chairs borrowed from the church hall like they were hymnals.

The porch lights glowed when they pulled in. His father climbed out first, clapping his hands as if to announce their arrival. Van slid from the back seat, balancing two hot casseroles while his mother piled a tin of cookies and a bag of wrapped gifts onto his load.

"Van," his father called, turning back at the steps, "don't forget the cooler and that sack of presents. Make yourself useful."

Van adjusted the casseroles, one slipping dangerously. "My hands are full, Dad." The words came sharper than he meant. "You've got two empty ones. Why can't you help?"

The air thinned. Emmalee froze with the cookie tin halfway to her chest.

His father's jaw flexed. "Watch that tone, boy."

Before it could snap, his mother slid past, brittle and brisk. "That's enough. We're at your uncle's. Let's get inside." She lifted the cooler herself, lips pressed tight.

Van swallowed, arms burning, and followed. His father

strode ahead as though nothing had been said, but inside Van something had shifted; he hadn't swallowed the words this time.

Dinner unfolded like always—less about food and more about Leslie's running commentary.

"Van, fetch the rolls."

"Van, take these plates to the kitchen."

"Van, pass the butter to your uncle."

Each command stacked on the last until Van felt like hired help. His father watched with satisfaction, as if all this fetching proved something upright about both of them.

Conversation circled menus. Leslie set Christmas breakfast at her house: egg casseroles, cinnamon rolls, fruit trays. His mom added lists for Christmas lunch. Folding chairs—how many? Who would pray? Who would carve? Van tuned it out.

He found Emmalee near the tree—Leslie's flawless ornaments framing photographs of Grandma at a dozen Christmases, eyes bright in moments that still breathed inside Van's chest.

"Remember how she'd sneak us chocolate drops before dinner?" Em whispered.

Van smiled, the ache warming for a second. "And wink like it was the biggest secret in the world."

They stood side by side, letting the faces in the frames steady them.

By dessert, Van had already gathered coats from the hall closet, stacking them on his arm. His father caught him at the door. "Trying to rush us along, are ya?" he laughed, rough and sharp.

"Figured I'd save you the energy of yelling at me to get them," Van said evenly, "and the wait."

Uncle David coughed into his fist. Leslie's laugh didn't land. His mother guided Emmalee out, eyes on the floor.

No one spoke again until the car rolled into their driveway and the engine cut. Then his father let it loose.

"You think you're funny? Smarting off in front of your uncle. Making me look like a fool."

"I wasn't smarting off. I was just—"

"Don't you talk back," he snapped. The car shuddered into park. "You think because you've got wheels, you're grown? Keys."

Van blinked. "What?"

"Your car keys. You'll ride with us to church tomorrow. Maybe the next day. You'll learn respect the hard way."

The metal bit his palm when he pulled them from his pocket. He wanted to refuse, wanted to run, but under his father's stare he opened his hand.

The keys jingled once when they left him. "That's what I thought," his father said, slipping them into his pocket.

Inside, the house exhaled casserole and pine. At dinner the next night, no one mentioned the keys. At church, Van sat stiff in the family pew, his father's voice booming through every hymn like he'd written them. He wore his pride like a cloak. Van felt like a prop.

He cracked his eyes during the prayer.

Across the aisle, Jeremiah's were open, too.

Just a flicker, but it found something in Van he hadn't been able to reach alone. Jeremiah didn't look away.

Van closed his eyes because he had to. The echo of that look stayed, pulsing like a small, stubborn light.

CHAPTER 21

CANDLELIGHT
AND MISTLETOE

The sanctuary air was thick and sweet, heavy with pine and the starch of a hundred polished shirts. Greenery laced every window, velvet softened the pulpit's edges, and poinsettias bled crimson along the altar like a slow tide. Shoulders brushed shoulders, packed tight in the pews as the choir rose, the first chord a low, rolling breath. When the soloist stretched "O Holy Night" into something grand and trembling, the sniffles rippled through the room right on cue. Van didn't sing. *My throat is cinched,* he thought, *tight with a different kind of silence.*

He and Jeremiah stood at the pulpit for the youth readings. The cloth of their sleeves brushed, a low current in the high room. *Don't look at him, don't you dare look,* Van thought. Jeremiah went first, voice steady, as though he had been born in that very spot. Van followed, words he had known since childhood weighing heavier in his mouth now. When he finished, his father's approving nod landed like a stamp. *It's just another performance for him,* Van realized, feeling the silent current of connection between him and Jeremiah tighten anyway.

A river of small flames began its journey down the pews. Van's father lit his with a solemn, practiced care, passing the light to Emmalee. When Van cupped his own candle, his hands trembled. Across the aisle, Jeremiah lifted his flame, his lips curving—barely a smile, but not nothing either. "Silent Night" rose, a hushed anthem, and Jeremiah's eyes were locked on his, unwavering. The final note floated and dropped into an abrupt quiet of breath and coughs. Then, his father's hand landed heavy on his shoulder. "That's my boy," he murmured, a gesture weighed down by performance.

The church spilled into the cold, dark air. Van bent to zip Emmalee's coat when a brush of warmth slid across his shoulder. Jeremiah was passing with his family, and he slowed, pulling the moment out.

"Good service," Jeremiah murmured, eyes flicking sideways. The words were not the point.

Van's "Yeah" was smaller than he intended.

His mother's voice cut through the air, sharp and bright: "Jeremiah, come on!" He gave the slightest tilt of his head and was gone.

The Shelton house throbbed when they got home, every room swelling with perfume, cologne, and the breath-heat of too many casseroles. Voices overlapped, a dull roar of praise for the soloist and gossip about the New Year's revival tally. Church and family blurred until they were indistinguishable. Van heard his name used as proof on a dozen tongues without being spoken to once, standing invisible in the kitchen doorway.

Then the front door creaked open, and Dana blew in, her grin bright enough to flip a breaker. "Lord have mercy, Van Shelton," she announced loud enough to turn heads, "if you fetch one more tray of deviled eggs I'm putting you in an apron and calling you the hired help." She looked up at Van with a face that said *I see you*, and the knot in his chest loosened a notch.

Orders flew like scattered birds:

"Van, more chairs!"

"Van, candles are low!"

"Van, grab those trays!"

Dana rolled her eyes dramatically. "What is this, the Van Shelton Slave Auction? Y'all know he's not the only one with legs, right?"

Across the way, Jeremiah's gaze found Van and lingered.

The old sprig of mistletoe hung in the hallway arch, its ribbon frayed, berries chipped. Van ended up beneath it, and Jeremiah stepped into the space, holding empty cups that didn't need to be carried anywhere.

"You missed a spot," Jeremiah said casually, nodding toward a candle behind Van.

Van realized where they were standing, the blood rushing hot to his neck. *Oh God, no.*

Jeremiah's smile tilted crooked. "Guess tradition says..."

Aunt Shelia's laugh rang out then, light enough to be a joke, strong enough to be permission. Laughter bubbled, someone whistled, but underneath, an older cousin muttered into his cup, "Boys don't kiss boys," loud enough to sting.

Jeremiah leaned in a fraction, his whisper a low current: "You okay with this?"

Van swallowed. "Yeah."

Jeremiah's fingers brushed his, a quick, hidden touch, and then he kissed Van's cheek—light, quick, a match striking fire inside Van's chest.

Across the room, his mother went pale, eyes flicking from Jeremiah's family to her husband, panic racing ahead of the moment. She hissed at Shelia: "I cannot believe you encouraged that—in my house—".

Shelia didn't even flinch. She leaned close, smile sugar, words steel: "In your house, that boy just smiled for the first time in weeks. If you can't be glad for that, maybe hush before you embarrass yourself."

Later, when the crowd thinned and the house sagged with exhaustion, Jeremiah appeared in the hallway doorway, a thought becoming a person.

"Busy night," he said softly.

"Feels like they'd forget to breathe if I didn't remind them," Van replied.

"You did good up there reading," Jeremiah added. He hesitated, then went quieter: "It didn't feel fake to me."

Van looked up. All the quiet glances, the shoulder brushes, the seconds stolen lived in the space between them.

"I meant it under the mistletoe," Jeremiah whispered softly. "Wasn't just playing along. I don't know what this is supposed to look like. I just know... I want it to be you".

Laughter spilled down the hall; Jeremiah stepped back, eyes burning. "I should go. See you."

Van watched him cross the frosty drive and climb into the passenger seat, taillights bleeding away into the night.

When the door shut on the last guest, the house finally went quiet enough to hear his father's heavy breathing. He paced the living room, building his anger like a sermon.

"Tonight was supposed to be about the birth of our Savior," he said, words sharp. "And what do I see? My son making a spectacle—smirking under mistletoe with the pastor's boy."

"It was a joke," his mother offered, voice thin. "Just kids."

"Don't you tell me what I saw." He turned on Van. "You embarrassed this family. In front of half the church."

Van stood, his fists tight, but his voice stayed level. "All I did was stand there. You're the one turning it into something more."

"Don't get smart," his father snapped. He pulled out the

BMW keys and thudded them onto the table. "You don't get these back until you learn respect."

His mother wiped her eyes with a dish towel and couldn't meet Van's gaze. Van held his father's stare until the man looked away first, stalking down the hall, the door closing harder than it needed to.

In bed, the house finally dark, the streetlight drew pale bars on his ceiling. It was Christmas Eve, the night that was supposed to be holy and bright. All he could hear was his own heartbeat, too big for his chest. He closed his eyes and saw Jeremiah's face instead of his father's. The memory of the kiss felt like a gift—something in the house that couldn't be taken.

He whispered into the dark, voice ragged: "God, I don't know if You're listening tonight. Maybe... maybe let Grandma hear me instead?" He swallowed. "I think I like Jeremiah... No, I know I do. And tonight it felt good. Not broken. Just... real. Like something she'd smile at".

He woke to the sound of a whisper: "Van?". Emmalee sat on the edge of his bed, looking small in her flannel nightgown.

"Merry Christmas," she said softly.

Van rubbed his eyes, forcing a tired smile. "Merry Christmas, Em."

They sat in silence for a while, holding onto each other in the quiet before the day unraveled.

"I don't like Christmas without her," she whispered.

"Me neither."

Down the hall, his mother's sharp, clipped voice drifted—already fussing about the schedule, about making sure everything was "just so". Emmalee sighed, burrowing closer: "I wish we could stay in here all day".

"Me too," he lied gently, because he knew better. The

house was already stirring, preparing for the day's performance.

The living room glowed with colored lights from the tree, the piles of wrapped boxes waiting like props in a play. His mother appeared, already dressed: "All right, let's go ahead and start. Van, grab the camera. We'll need pictures with each gift". His father shuffled in behind her, sinking into the recliner like a stone meant to sink, his anger from the night before curdling into silence.

Van handed Emmalee the first present. She grinned at the plastic doll.

"Hold it up, Emmalee," his mother said, voice sharp. The flash went off. Click. Proof.

Another gift: clothes. The smile dimmed.

"Hold it up," his mother said. Another flash. Click. Proof.

Van's pile held the usual mix, a book he didn't ask for, an outdated stereo system.

"Hold it up," his mother said again. He did. Click. Proof.

Each gift was documented, then hurriedly moved into piles. Open, pose, pack away. By the time the last ribbon was tossed into the trash bag, his mother was glancing at the clock: "We've got an hour to be at David and Leslie's. Everyone needs to be ready."

At Uncle David and Aunt Leslie's, the air churned with cinnamon and bacon. The dining room groaned under the weight of casseroles and biscuits. Every detail was staged, every napkin straightened by Aunt Leslie, who stood at the head of the table like a conductor. The performance of breakfast began.

Each bite came with commentary; compliments rolled like rehearsed lines. Van ate quietly, the chatter buzzing around him like static. The breakfast wasn't about food or family; it was rehearsal, proof the Sheltons could still look the part.

Then Cousin Amelia leaned across the table, her sing-song

sharpened for effect: "Sooo... heard there was a festive moment under the mistletoe last night." Eyebrows bounced. "Between Van and the pastor's boy."

Forks paused. Heads tilted. Uncle David cleared his throat: "Amelia." It was warning and weariness in one word.

The deacon's wife, who had mysteriously stayed for breakfast, couldn't help herself. "Boys will be boys," she said tightly. "Still, we must be mindful what we model in mixed company."

Aunt Leslie's smile went porcelain. "It was nothing," she announced for the room. "Just holiday foolishness."

His mother adjusted a napkin that didn't need adjusting. "Let's move on," she murmured, voice too light to hide the strain.

His father didn't look at Van. He didn't have to. The set of his mouth wrote the rest.

Van felt the heat crawl up his neck, but kept his voice level. "It was a joke. Like Aunt Leslie said." He lifted his glass. "Now can someone pass the biscuits?" The room exhaled, and conversation limped back to safe ground.

By the time breakfast was over, Van already felt wrung out, but the day wasn't finished. The family reconvened at the Shelton house for lunch. When the seats were stuffed and the plates were full, Uncle David cleared his throat. "Well. Somebody ought to bless the food".

Eyes shifted to Van. His mother's gaze cut across the table, pinning him: *Do it.*

So he stood.

The familiar Baptist blessing spilled from his lips at first, automatic as breathing. "Heavenly Father, thank You for this day, for the food we are about to receive, bless the hands that prepared it—"

Stomachs growled, forks twitched. The ritual moved toward its end.

But Van stopped. He opened his eyes a sliver. Heads were bowed, lids shut. A room full of people who wouldn't see him say it.

"Lord..." he began again. He spoke about the empty chair, about missing his grandmother, and the fear of saying it out loud. His voice broke, but he pressed on, ending the prayer: "Bless this family with honesty. With love that's bigger than appearances. With memories that don't fade just because we're too scared to speak them out loud. Amen".

The word hung there in the full, thick, holy silence. Scattered "Amens" followed. Then, the clatter resumed like a machine restarting—napkins, forks, the safe hum of small talk.

Van sat down slow, his pulse still hot in his throat. No one looked directly at him, not even Emmalee, whose little hand brushed against his under the table in a quick squeeze. *I heard you. I needed that too.* His father ate mechanically, jaw tight. His mother's glance brushed him, lingering a heartbeat too long—caught between a warning and a thanks.

He knew he'd cracked something open. Maybe just for himself. Maybe for Emmalee. He ate what was in front of him and tasted none of it, yet inside, there was a strange steadiness, a strange relief. He felt the ache, yes, but for the first time in weeks, he also felt the warmth. And that was enough to carry him through the rest of Christmas Day.

"Ritual without love is just procedure."

———VAN'S JOURNAL

CHAPTER 22
FIRST BELL, NEW LINES

The first-day bell didn't ring so much as ricochet—down the freshly waxed hall, through doorways propped with textbooks, off lockers still sweating August. The whole building smelled like pencil shavings and a storm that never quite broke.

Van moved with the current and tried not to get pulled under. Someone had taped the JV football schedule across the trophy case; last year's team photo grinned through the curling edges. The tryout sheet flapped below, paper breathing in the air conditioning. **COLBY THOMAS**—in all caps—sat near the top and had been circled twice in red, a touch of Coach Thomas even on the sign-up list.

"Donovan Shelton." Dana slid in beside him, already in mid-hustle, braid over one shoulder, new sneakers squeaking. "Quit loitering with ghosts. Mrs. Whitaker will sacrifice us to Lauridsen if we're late."

They passed freshmen hunted by their schedules and couples already claiming corners by the vending machines. The music wing felt cooler, older, like a sanctuary had been grafted into a school. Inside the choir room, an upright piano held court. Along the wall, black folders slept in cubbies labeled in Mrs. Whitaker's neat hand. **MISSUS WHITAKER** was pressed into a brass plate on her office door, as if she'd arrived like that.

She stood at the piano in a navy shirtwaist and pearls, her hair in a French twist that had never once fought back. "Good morning, choristers," she said, a greeting that sounded like plucked strings. "Folders by section. Tenors—breathe with dignity, not desperation. We are not rescuing kittens from a well."

A few sophomores snickered. Mrs. Whitaker pressed a triad that settled the room like a prayer.

A boy Van didn't know slid into the row in front of him and turned like he'd been joining this conversation all summer. Denim jacket sleeves shoved to the elbows, thin chain at his throat, a small black stud catching the fluorescent light. Confident, not cocky; the difference felt like posture more than volume.

"Tariq," he said. "Transferred in from West. Is your director as terrifying as her reputation?"

"More," Dana stage-whispered. "She's also omniscient."

Van found his own voice. "She reads pitch the way other people read palms."

Tariq grinned. "Mystic. I can work with that. If my tenor drifts, tug me back by the soul."

Mrs. Whitaker clapped a crisp pattern. Scales vaulted the room. Breath, vowel, vowel, vowel. When someone tried to hum, she lifted one eyebrow without breaking tempo and the humming died of natural causes.

The door sighed open in the second arpeggio. Jeremiah slipped in with a muttered sorry and that lithe way of moving that made even apologies feel athletic. His hair had gone longer over the summer; it curled at his collar in a shape Pastor Rich tolerated and Denise smoothed when she could. He lifted a hand without thinking—hello but smaller—and Van felt it land across the room. Jeremiah took a back-row folder and slid into the music like he'd never left it.

By fourth period, the school had drawn its lines again. In English, desks made continents, and the teacher made them colonize. In Algebra II, someone chalked a problem so long it was basically a short story. At lunch, Colby appeared with grass stains and a grin that looked earned. "First cuts Thursday," he announced, dropping onto the bench. "I ran a four-point-some-thing and Coach said, 'Don't slow down, Thomas,' which I'm choosing to hear as love."

"Or obligation," Dana said sweetly. "How's your hamstring, prince?"

"It's fine," he said, and then winced. "It's not fine. It will be fine."

Jeremiah showed up late with a tray and a soccer bag that thumped its own introduction. He slid into the seat across from Van like he didn't plan to stay and did anyway. "Varsity meets with coaches after school," he said, like it was a fact and not a thing that had been earned with sweat. "First match in two weeks."

Tariq appeared at the end of the bench and took up space like he'd been invited. "Is this the arts-and-athletics coalition? Gorgeous. I brought contraband." He produced a sleeve of Oreos, opened them with a magician's flourish, and offered the row.

"Careful," Dana murmured. "He'll steal your heart and your conditioner."

"Just the conditioner," Tariq said. "Hearts are high main-tenance."

They were still laughing when the bell split the room and the world re-sorted them.

After school, Van found the parking lot, heat shimmering

over the windshields like a mirage of lake water. The BMW sat crooked between two chalked lines, a minor rebellion that made him smile until he caught sight of the license plate again —**THANKS DAD!**—and the smile curdled.

He got home to his father in the kitchen, standing like a man who'd been waiting to deliver news to a captive press. "Big day," he said, brandishing a church flier. "Youth lock-in Friday. They asked for help and I told 'em the Sheltons would show up."

Van opened the fridge and let the cold air stall him. "Who asked?"

"Don't matter. I volunteered." His father slapped the counter with triumph. "We're a unit, son. Get used to it."

Something like gratitude and dread tangled in Van's chest. "I've got work," he said. "Friday night shift. I told Marlene weeks ago."

His father's mouth flattened, then re-inflated into performance. "We'll make it work. They need a man who can hang with boys without letting 'em run wild." He winked at Van like they shared a joke. "You'll be fine. I'll keep 'em off your back."

Van looked at his mother, who was measuring rice and measuring her words. She lifted one shoulder in a gesture that meant *later*. Aunt Shelia's voice lived somewhere in the corners of their house like wind around eaves: *Don't make him perform love. Make him do it.*

Van went to his room and lay on the bed until the ceiling made sense. At school, breath had filled his ribs and made sound. At home, he was part of a chorus of one.

CHAPTER 23

CHAPERONES
AND PUNCHLINES

The gym was already humid by the time Van arrived for the lock-in. Pizza boxes towered like a city no one planned. A string of Christmas lights blinked in one corner where someone had tried to make ambience out of a ball rack. The sound system kept sacrificing the beat to static.

Van hauled two-liters to the drink table. Dana was setting out paper cups with the diligence of a surgeon. "You see the volunteer list?" she asked, mouth tight. "Your dad signed up for everything except 'No.'"

"Don't," Van said. "Not yet."

His father swept in five minutes later wearing a whistle like a medal. "Troops!" he boomed, clapping once, twice, and then more because the sound pleased him. Heads turned. That was the point. "We're gonna have righteous fun, which is to say— no kissing, no hiding, no climbing the bleachers like mountain goats, and absolutely no... whatever nonsense y'all picked up off those music videos."

Groans. Snickering. Someone said "It's called *MTV*, Mr. Shelton," and his father grinned like he'd planned the line. He slung an arm around Van's shoulders and squeezed like a headlock.

"This one here," he told the cluster of boys near the half court line, "he's my canary. If Van can survive the night, all y'all pass."

Laughter. The kind that puts weight on the person it points at.

"Dad," Van said, quick. It wasn't a plea. It was a boundary drawn with a pencil—thin and erasable, but there.

"He knows I'm kidding," his father said to nobody in particular. "He cries at Hallmark commercials."

The whistle thumped Van's cheek when his father bounced away. The joke vaulted. Some boys repeated it. Others filed it for later. Van's face went hot then cold.

Across the gym, Jeremiah had paused under the scoreboard with the JV boys. He watched without moving his mouth. Dana had frozen with a stack of plates, eyes flicking in Van's direction like a lighthouse—*for you, for you, for you.*

The evening unspooled in loud waves: dodgeball like war, four-square like diplomacy, a worship set that couldn't choose a tempo. In the kitchen, Van rinsed cups and listened to the laughter his father aimed like a spotlight at himself. By ten, Mr. Shelton was a cruise director. By midnight, the spotlight dimmed, the whistle hung around his neck like a surrender, and he vanished to the fellowship hall to "help with cleanup." Van passed him leaning in the doorway, talking big to another dad and thumbing through last month's church newsletter like it was urgent business.

Near one a.m., Youth Pastor Lane dimmed the lights and gave a devotional that drifted from temptation to politics to the sin of skinny jeans. Van's lungs shrank. He slipped into the hallway and leaned his forehead against the cinderblock. It was cool, thank God, and real.

Footsteps. Not his father's echo. His mother's low heels, sure and familiar. She took the spot beside him, shoulder a breath away.

"He loves you," she said, which was her way of saying *I'm sorry*. "He doesn't know how to do it without an audience."

Van's laugh came out like paper tearing. "Then he needs to practice when the seats are empty."

She nodded, slow. "I told him he was being unkind without meaning to."

"Meaning doesn't change how it lands."

Her mouth twitched. "Shelia is waiting in the kitchen. She's... sharpening her words."

As if conjured, Aunt Shelia turned the corner carrying a roll of paper towels like a scepter. "Where's your daddy?" she asked Van.

"Checking the integrity of the snack table," Van said.

"Mm." Shelia adjusted her grip on the roll. "I asked him who he is when nobody's looking. He didn't like the question."

"Most people don't," Van said.

She squeezed his shoulder, the way you steady a ladder before a man climbs. "You're not a prop. Don't let him set you on a stage without your permission."

By three, the gym had a smell that made Van swear he'd never own carpet. By five, the last game collapsed into a pile of limbs that might have been sleep. At sunrise, they stumbled outside for a group photo. Mr. Shelton re-materialized, one arm around Van, smile polished.

"Good for the church page," he said, though he didn't run it.

On the drive home, the car was a different quiet than usual. No talk radio. No replayed jokes.

"Fun night," his father ventured, fishing.

"The kids had fun," Van said. "You had an audience."

"You watch your tone, son."

"I am," Van said, the words surprising him with their steadiness. "That's why I'm saying it."

His father's jaw flexed. He made a noise that wasn't a word. When they pulled into the driveway, his mother was waiting on the porch with two mugs. She handed one to Van, then turned to her husband.

"Maybe sit the next one out," she said, gentle but edged.

"We'll see," he deflected—which meant *not unless there's a crowd to see me not.*

He went inside. The screen door clacked. His mother watched it, then looked at Van. "You did good," she said. "Not performance. Presence."

"I'm so tired," he said.

"Go sleep," she said, and kissed his forehead like it was still allowed.

CHAPTER 24

AFTER THE FINAL WHISTLE

A Thursday wind ran its fingers across the soccer field and left the night smelling like rain that might keep its promise. Moths orbited the stadium lights like faithful things. Van and Dana climbed to the top row of the bleachers where the metal hummed with every stomp below.

Jeremiah settled into the first half like a song he'd known in another life. He didn't force it—didn't chest-thump or glare or shout. He just kept finding space where there shouldn't be any. When the ball slipped to his feet along the wing, he lifted his head, saw something he liked, and sent a low strike skimming just inside the far post like he'd whispered to it and it listened.

The bench erupted. Jeremiah didn't. He just turned, cheeks flushed, and let his eyes climb the bleachers until they found Van. The look wasn't a grin. It was a confession: *I hoped you saw.*

Across campus, JV football spat out disappointment. Colby arrived with his helmet in the crook of his arm and his socks rolled down like surrender flags. He took the row below, elbows on his knees, stare on the field because pride demanded it.

"Coach says adversity builds character," he said without introducing himself to the moment.

"Your character must be absolutely jacked," Dana said, handing him half her nachos.

He laughed once, a bark that hurt to hear. "Shut up."

"Love you too."

Stillwater pressed late. Our keeper punched away something dangerous. The ref swallowed the whistle when he should've coughed it. Van watched Jeremiah watch the clock and breathe careful.

Game. The buzzer sounded more like a sigh than a shout. 2–1. Hands slapped hands. Cleats scuffed a victory language across the track.

Under the music wing's eaves, the air felt different—cooler, lonelier, as if the building kept its own secrets by the HVAC. The yellow security light buzzed with a moth's stubborn theology: try again, try again, try again.

Van put his head back against the bricks and counted the beats of a heart that had lost its place. The door eased open and didn't click shut. Jeremiah slid through sideways, jersey hem tugged down, hair damp, grin shy and not.

"Hi," he said, and the word landed like the first note played true after a bar of noise.

"Hi." Van's mouth forgot its job; his hands remembered it and found his pockets.

They stood in that half-space—too close to be casual, too far to be a lie. Jeremiah reached like he might brush a leaf off Van's shoulder, then thought better and tucked his hand back into his sleeve. They both stepped in, then both stepped back, then both laughed, which broke whatever bruise the night had made.

"I keep writing sentences and deleting them," Jeremiah said, eyes on the wedge of light under the door. "I don't know how to say the thing I want without it sounding like a movie."

"Say it wrong," Van said. "I'll hear it right."

"That," Jeremiah said, "is not fair." He looked up. His eyes glinted the way hymnals sometimes do right before the choir ruins you. "I wanted to kiss you in June." A beat. "I want to kiss you now."

"Okay," Van said, and felt every muscle try to leave his body and stay at once.

They came together wrong first: a knock of nose, a stifled laugh caught in a mouth. Jeremiah whispered "sorry" against Van's lips and the apology moved them from wrong to right. The second press was small and certain and not the end of the world, which is what made it feel like one beginning.

There weren't fireworks. There was a breath they didn't realize they were sharing until they needed to stop to take another. There was warmth carried up through fingertips into places that had been cold too long. There was a moth smacking the light, stubborn in its desire, and the two of them smiling into each other's mouths at the ridiculousness of being creatures who fly at brightness even when it burns.

Jeremiah rested his forehead against Van's because walls were echoey and foreheads were not. "We don't have to name it here," he said. "We can name it where we can keep it safe."

"Okay," Van said. "But I'm going to remember this here."

"Me too." Jeremiah's thumb found the hinge of Van's jaw like it had been given directions. "Sonic?"

Van had forgotten cars and food and the concept of the world. "In ten."

They walked out separately, because muscle memory makes cowards and survivors of us both. At the curb, they converged again, laughing too loud when Dana lobbed a ketchup packet at them through the open window. Colby sat on the truck tailgate with his ankles crossed and his ego trying to unknot. Seth held court about nothing, which was his specialty. Tariq sauntered up late, dropped a photocopied page of "Shenandoah" on the table, and tapped a pencil note he'd scrawled along the margin: **tell your lover boy i approve of his vowels (trust me, i'm a professional).**

Van tried not to grin and failed.

No one asked why Van looked like he'd been breathing better air. No one asked why Jeremiah's smile kept showing up then getting contained. The group had its own mythology: wins, losses, fries hot, shakes too thin, the way the floodlights made all of them look a little kinder than they felt.

On the drive home, Van put both hands at ten and two because his body needed something to do with itself besides levitate. Dana sang harmonies on the radio that weren't there. Tariq, from the back seat, said, "If you two ever need coaching, I do seminars," and then cackled when Van nearly missed the turn.

Van went to sleep with the moth behind his eyelids and a kiss on his mouth. He dreamed about neither and woke tasting both.

"If they lock you out of the sanctuary, look for God in the kitchen."

———GRANDMA

CHAPTER 25
THE HOUSE WITH ALL THE LIGHTS OFF

The night he found her lamp in his living room, it didn't matter that he'd just counted tips and washed coffee out of his hair. It didn't matter that he'd bagged two orders of fried okra for a man who said "bless you" like a threat. All that mattered was the way emerald glass threw patched light across the Shelton couch as if it had always belonged on that end table.

Her cedar chest had materialized beneath the front window, too. The floral painting from over her sofa now hung where the family portrait used to be, the nail holes spackled like erasures. Van's body knew the shapes; his mind did not.

His mother was polishing the edges of something that didn't need polishing. "We went over," she said, too bright. "While you were at work. Leslie said if we didn't start we never would."

"You went through her things." The words fell like he'd dropped them from his mouth by accident.

"We sorted," his father corrected, eyes on the TV. "Family took family things. Don't get sentimental."

Van stared at the lamp. He could hear the click of its chain in a room that wasn't this one. "You could have called me."

"You were working," his father said, as if a clock was a reason and not a convenience. "Anyway, there's plenty left. Drive over and pick through what's there before Leslie hauls it to the charity shop."

The phrase *pick through* made Van feel like an animal at a carcass. He swallowed what he wanted to say because there were too many words to pick through, too, and none of them would land right. He reached for his keys and didn't slam the door because the part of him that was raised in that woman's kitchen wouldn't let him.

The porch light at his grandmother's house used to click on at the first crunch of tires. It didn't. The driveway felt longer, the grass an intent darker than the rest of the night, the windows exact rectangles of nothing. He let himself in with the key she'd pressed into his palm at thirteen with a wink and a "Now don't lock yourself out of my heart, baby."

The house was colder than outside. It smelled like lemon cleaner and yesterday. In the living room, emptiness had a shape. The spot where the coffee table had sat was a square of rug matted into a memory of weight. The quilt ladder leaned naked against the wall, dust stripes where color had been. Post-it notes —tilted, relentless—bloomed from the last of the furniture: **CHARITY. TRASH. KEEP—DAVID. KEEP—LESLIE. CHARITY.**

In the kitchen, the fridge hummed its devotion to a power bill no one would pay much longer. Its door was bald—no children's drawings, no recipes with grease kisses, no magnet collection from towns she'd loved for a weekend. The sink was dry. A single rinsed mug—plain white, hairline crack, lipstick ghost—sat upside down on a towel like it had chosen dignity.

He walked because his feet knew the tour: here the phone

where she'd sat to hear the news that wasn't news; here the hallway photos that were rectangles of lighter paint now; here the bedroom where the quilt had always been turned down just enough to suggest a nap. The dresser drawers stood open like mouths mid-story. The top one held a fan of Sunday school bookmarks, a rubber band fossilized into a stretched-out eight, two pennies and a scrap of paper with a verse he could hear her saying (Micah 6:8, of course).

In the laundry room, behind the door, a metal folding chair leaned with dust on it like a secret. He pulled it into the living room and opened it in the place where his shins had bruised themselves on the coffee table a hundred times. He sat. The chair squealed under his weight, then settled into a more companionable silence.

"Okay," he said to the room that had known him better than any man ever would. "Okay."

He tried to find the God he could talk to without feeling managed. Not the God from Lane's handouts with ten bullet points and a cartoon lamb. Not the God from the pulpit whose anger could always find a target with a rainbow on it. The God his grandmother had breathed to while stirring gravy, who had lived in the soft dip of her mattress when she set aside her Bible and listened with her whole skin.

"I don't know how to keep the parts of me together," he said, and the room didn't flinch. "I'm trying to be a Christian. I'm still a Baptist whether I like the word or not. I'm trying to be a good son and a decent brother and a person who doesn't roll his eyes when people say 'guard your heart' like it's a garage door. I'm trying to be me—and I don't know how to be all of that when the people who taught me how to pray keep saying the part of me that tells the truth about love is the part that cancels the rest."

He let it sit. The fridge thunked softly. Something settled in the attic the way old houses do when they exhale.

"They say there's a plan," he went on, voice fraying and then knitting itself back together. "A plan for my purity, my thoughts, my friends, my future wife who has a name in heaven that I am supposed to learn to want. They say if I feel something else, it's temptation, not truth; it's a test, not a map. But what if the test is whether I can tell You the truth and keep telling it? What if the plan is not a fence but a path I have to keep walking without knowing what's past the turn?"

He could hear Mrs. Whitaker in his head, too—*breathe from the ribs, not the throat*—and tried it. The room seemed to like him better when he did.

"Grandma," he said, and the air changed temperature by a degree only he would notice. "If you can hear me, if heaven has visiting hours, if God lets you put your ear to the floor and listen —do that now. Because I'm going to say it, and when I say it, I want you to hear it first."

He looked at the spot on the rug where her feet had found the same place every morning because habit is how we learn to love. He looked at the door where she'd hugged him with her cheek and whispered, *You take my blessing with you or you don't leave at all.*

"I'm gay," he said. The word didn't echo. It didn't shatter. It arrived and sat down, polite, like it had been invited and just needed to be told where to put its coat.

"I'm gay," he said again, because the first time had been for the house and the second could be for God. "And I want to follow You. And I want to love in a way that doesn't break me in half. And I want to stop apologizing to my empty room for the shape of the truth."

He waited for shame to come around the corner, late but eager. What arrived instead was his grandmother at the stove, humming "Come Thou Fount" slightly off-key, saying *Listen between the sounds, baby. That's where He lives.*

Van leaned forward, elbows on his knees, palms together like prayer or begging, which is sometimes the same thing. "If the church tells me there's no place for me, I'm going to look around and see if You're still there anyway. And if You are, I'm staying with You. And if You aren't—well, I don't believe that. I don't. So please—help me keep believing that the table You set is bigger than the one they're guarding."

He sat until his back ached and the metal chair left its rungs on his thighs. He stood and walked the tour again, slower this time, touching doorframes the way people touch stones at places that have been holy to other people for a long time.

In the bottom dresser drawer, under hymnals with brittle spines and a fan of bulletin corners, he found her recipe box. The lid was cracked; the cards were greasy with love. Fried chicken—oil (not too much), salt (pinch), don't crowd the skillet. The chocolate pie with the meringue he'd begged for at twelve—beat the whites until they stand up like they're proud.

On the bookshelf there was a green hymnbook he'd carried for her hands when hers shook. In the margins of "Come Thou Fount," she'd drawn a tiny heart. Beside "Great Is Thy Faithfulness," she'd written three names and three dates, each one the day someone had come home after too long gone.

He took the hymnbook and the recipe box because stealing from the dead isn't stealing if they wanted you to have it. He closed the front door and waited out of habit for the porch light to come on, and when it didn't, he still lifted his chin like something warm had just touched it.

Back at the Shelton house, the emerald lamp threw new light on old walls. His father yawned through a rerun and didn't wonder where Van had been. His mother folded a napkin into another square and then another until it wouldn't fold anymore.

"How was it?" she asked, eyes on her hands.

"Quiet," he said. "And loud."

He took the hymnbook to his room, set it on the dresser, and slid the recipe box under his bed like contraband and comfort. He brushed his fingers over the hymnbook's worn title. *Come Thou Fount.* He whispered the old line into the dark, not because he needed saving from himself, but because he wanted to learn how to sing his own name and God's in the same breath without going hoarse.

Here I raise mine Ebenezer.

Here by Thy great help I've come.

CHAPTER 26
BREATH AND NOISE

The pep rally tasted like rubber and sugar—gym floor varnish and cotton candy that had no business being inside a school. A drumline rattled the bleachers until everyone clapped whether they meant it or not. Cheer bows bobbed like punctuation marks.

Colby jogged out with JV like he'd been waiting to hear his name over a loudspeaker his whole life. "Let's go!" he yelled, chest up, jaw set, soaking it in. Coach Thomas met him with a meaty high-five and that half-grin that meant *son, you're mine* even if he'd never say it that clearly.

Across the gym, the soccer boys leaned on the rail like they'd been cast in a quieter movie. Jeremiah stood among them, shoulders loose, eyes more sky than storm. He didn't look around until he did, and when he did, he found Van up in the bleachers. It was quick. It still hit.

"Lord, deliver me," Dana said, fanning herself with the program like a deacon's wife. "If they say 'make some noise' one more time, I'll make a scene."

Van laughed through his nose. "You always make a scene."

"Correct." She bumped his arm. "After-school Sonic? I need tater tots to recover from school spirit."

By the time the vice principal finished the seventh reminder about "behavior expectations," the band had gasped itself out and the gym began to empty in heat-waves. Van and Dana slipped into the music wing where the air was cooler and the walls smelled like old stands and pencil shavings.

Mrs. Whitaker had already chalked the fall program on the board in her careful hand, each title squared like a promise.

"Breath is the currency with which you purchase *legato*," she said as they found folders. "Do not spend it like you've just been paid on Friday."

Tariq swanned in two minutes late, already talking. "My guidance counselor says I'm 'extra expressive.' I said, 'Yes, ma'am, I'm the sale rack with the best deals.' Hello, my darlings."

Mrs. Whitaker didn't look up from her pencil. "Mr. Reyes, please come in *under* the tempo."

"I will be demure," Tariq promised, crossing his heart. He stage-whispered to Van, "Demure is a limited-time offer."

Warm-ups slid into Palestrina. The room changed when they started—spines lengthened, laughter tucked itself into pockets, mouths went tall and tall again on the Latin.

"Stop devouring your 'u' like it owes you money," Mrs. Whitaker said mildly. "Place it and move along. Tenors, you are not first responders; you do not have to arrive early."

On the second pass she drifted, listening close enough to feel like a mirror. She stopped behind Van. Didn't speak. Didn't nod. Just stayed for half a phrase and walked on. Somehow that was better than a compliment.

At break, Tariq spun a chair backward and draped himself over it. "So. Your boy."

Van looked at the carpet. "We're not doing that here."

"We are absolutely doing that here," Tariq purred. "But fine, we'll whisper." He lowered his voice. "I like the way you look at him like you already wrote a song and haven't sung it yet."

"Rehearsal," Mrs. Whitaker called, and the spell broke.

They were halfway through "Sure on This Shining Night" when a shape filled the glass sliver in the door.

Van's father—palms on hips, grin like a billboard. He did an exaggerated tiptoe into the lobby, peeking in like a tourist. When the last chord cut and Mrs. Whitaker raised a hand for notes, the door cracked open.

"There he is—my little songbird." Mr. Shelton's voice hit the risers like a thrown tennis ball. A couple of chuckles, mostly because no one knew what else to do.

Mrs. Whitaker turned, only her eyes moving. "Mr. Shelton," she said, not sweet, not sharp, just level. "Inside voices in the music hall."

He blinked, then chuckled as if she'd made a joke for him. "Just picking him up. Big man's working these days."

"Borrowed for one more hour," she said, already back to the baton. "We are learning to spend our breath responsibly."

He held his hands up—*my bad*—but as he backed away he stage-whispered, "Don't faint on the high notes, son."

Tariq leaned just enough to murmur, "If you do, faint handsomely." Van focused on his measure numbers like they could save him.

After rehearsal, Jeremiah waited in the little side hall that always smelled like brass. He didn't touch Van, didn't even move, just walked beside him quietly like they were carrying a ladder between them.

"You looked like you wanted to fight the air," he said finally.

"I didn't want to be a joke," Van said.

"You're not," Jeremiah said. "You're the part of the song that makes the other parts behave."

Sonic was neon and salt and blessedly ordinary. They ate in the lot with the windows down. Tariq held up his straw like it was an art piece and intoned, "Hydration is gay culture," until Dana almost shot cherry limeade out her nose.

By the time Van clocked in at Magnolia, he'd talked himself down. He tied his apron, rolled silverware. Mr. Shelton came in during the second hour with a church buddy, said nothing to Van for ten minutes, then—when the buddy asked "He yours?" —clapped Van on the shoulder like a trophy.

"Best tenor in the county," he said. "Gets it from me."

Van refilled their coffee without looking up. "Need anything else?" he asked the buddy.

"We're good," the man said. Mr. Shelton nodded, satisfied, and turned back to his story. The laugh he used with friends sounded different, like he'd borrowed it.

Van took a tray to Booth Six and breathed like Mrs. Whitaker had taught him—slow in, smooth out—buying *legato* one measure at a time.

CHAPTER 27
THE HOUSE WITH ITS LIGHTS OFF

They called it a "touch base" in Aunt Leslie's call, which was cousin for *meeting where Leslie already decided.* The dining room filled: Uncle David with his quiet-sheriff gait; Leslie with a legal pad and a pen that clicked like a metronome; two aunts, one opinion each; Van's mother in her best smile; Aunt Shelia in a shirt that said DON'T MISTAKE MY SILENCE FOR AGREEMENT.

"We need to move briskly," Leslie began, as if briskness were a fruit of the Spirit. "The market is favorable. Estate sale for what remains. Family takes sentimental items this week, then donation pickup on Friday."

Van folded his hands so he wouldn't clench them. "What remains?"

"Everyone stopped by," Leslie said, reading her roll sheet. "People chose what they felt connected to. We wanted to keep momentum."

"I work," Van said. He kept his voice calm even while something pushed under his ribs. "Sometimes momentum could swing by after my shift."

His father didn't look up from his pie. "Plenty left," he said. "You can go pick through tonight if you want."

Shelia turned her head slowly. "We are not talking about the Target clearance rack," she said. "We are talking about—" her voice thinned for a heartbeat and came back flint— "a life."

Silence sat down at the head of the table and folded its hands.

Uncle David coughed. "The roof, Leslie. Don't forget the roof."

Van looked at his mother. She looked at her napkin. He swallowed. "I need... a walk-through," he said. "With Em. Not to snatch the best stuff like it's a yard sale. Just to say goodbye slow, to find the little things no one else would see."

Leslie's pen hovered, then sighed. "Tuesday evening," she said. "I'll make sure the alarm is off." It sounded like a permission slip and almost like care.

It didn't matter.

Tuesday evening came, and Magnolia ran behind, and the fryer broke, and a church bus clogged the turn lane. Van pulled into his parents' driveway after nine and stopped dead behind the taillight shine. The living room window glowed gold.

Inside: his grandmother's lamp. His grandmother's side table. The afghan she'd made with shades of green that didn't match on purpose, draped on his mother's couch like it had never loved another room.

"What the—" Van heard himself say aloud.

His mother was fixing a crooked picture frame like pictures could hold a house together. His father had the remote. The football game looked smug on the TV.

"Y'all went today," Van said, heartbeat suddenly in his palms. "Without me."

His father didn't mute the game. "We had a chance to get over there," he said. "Busy week. You can go tomorrow and pick through what's left. There's still plenty ain't worth a dime to anybody but you."

"That's... not the point," Van said. It came out thin. He cleared his throat. "You took the point and set it in our living room."

"Don't use that tone," his father warned, eyes still on the screen. "They're things, Van."

"Yeah," Van said, because the word snapped like a twig. "And they were hers. And maybe I wanted to be there when they weren't anymore."

"Lower your voice," his mother said softly—the way people say *please* when they don't want to cry. "Emmalee's asleep."

Van swallowed fire and turned it into motion. "I'm going," he said.

"Now?" his father scoffed. "It's late."

"Yeah," Van said again, but this time it meant *I'm tired of waiting until it's convenient for everyone but me.* He grabbed his keys.

The drive was muscle memory—left at the water tower, curve at the pecan grove, gravel pop as the tires took the driveway. Except when he cut the engine and the lights died, the house didn't wink its porch light at him from the kitchen like it always had. No soft square of yellow. Just dark windows staring back like old photographs.

He stood in the yard and listened to the kind of quiet that isn't peace. The kind that means something left.

The key turned heavy in the lock. The smell hit first—faint lemon oil under dust, a memory of Sunday roast pinned to the baseboards. The living room echoed when he stepped in, like he'd grown taller and the room hadn't.

Post-its blinked from the empties. **CHARITY. CHARITY. CHARITY.** The sofa's ghost was stamped into the carpet. The wall that used to hold the framed cross-stitch of Psalm 23 had a rectangle of paler paint where a life had shielded it from the sun.

He walked room to room like a tour guide he didn't want to be.

Kitchen: the drawer where she kept twist-ties was open and empty. One glass with lipstick halos waited in the sink. He didn't touch it.

Bedroom: the box fan still in the corner like a scarecrow on break. A wire hanger on the doorknob. The closet smelled like Yardley and wintergreen mints and the safety of a person who always kept tissues in her sleeve. A single cardigan slumped over a chair back. He lifted it and pressed his face to it and breathed like he'd been running.

Laundry room: the metal folding chair. The one she set up for shelling peas or resting between chores. He pulled it out, opened it in the dark living room, and sat.

"Okay," he said, to no one and to God. "What am I supposed to do with this?"

The house listened. He tried again.

"I don't want to be angry and I am. I don't want to be petty and I might be. I don't know how to feel like a good person when the church keeps saying the thing that makes me feel the most honest is the same thing that makes me... wrong."

He let the word sit. He didn't like it. He made it stay anyway.

"I love You," he said into the room that had hosted chicken dinners and Sunday naps. "Or I'm trying to. I love this... this boy." The word still felt dangerous and perfect. "When I'm with him I feel like I'm telling the truth with my whole body. Does that mean I can't be a Christian? Does that mean I can't be a Baptist the way she taught me? Because she taught me You listened to kids and fools and people who didn't know the right words yet. That You stayed."

Wind shivered the boxwood outside and scraped a branch

against the window like a fingernail. Somewhere in the house the clock ticked stubbornly on, refusing to learn new time.

"I want to be good," he said. "I also want to be whole. If those are the same thing, show me. If they're not, forgive me for choosing whole."

He sat until the metal bit crescents into the backs of his thighs and the house lost its edges and became only smell and ache and the rhythm of breath he finally remembered to count. On the way out, he took the green hymnbook she loved from a shelf the others had ignored and slid it under his arm. He straightened the doormat because she would have, locked the door, and waited—ridiculous—for the porch light that didn't come on.

"Some rooms are small so courage can fit."

———MRS. WHITAKER

CHAPTER 28

PRACTICE ROOM THREE

Rehearsal ended in a clap of folder rings. The hall outside the choir room clanged with lockers and laughter and the wet dog smell of football boys who ran the wrong way to showers. Van slipped through it like a note through a noisy bar.

Jeremiah leaned where the bass cabinets lived, head down, thumbs hooked in his backpack straps. He looked up with that small startled smile that always felt like a secret handshake.

"Three?" he asked. Meaning Practice Room Three. The small one with the emergency light that hummed like a cricket.

They ducked in. The door's click felt like a kind word.

"Hey," Jeremiah said, and his voice was soft enough that Van wanted to catch it and keep it. "I—" He laughed once, silently. "I'm not good at this."

"Me neither," Van said. His hands didn't know where to go, so he put one flat on the wall. The fabric panel gave under his palm and held him like a seatbelt.

Jeremiah stepped close like a person approaching a deer that might run. "Can I—?" He winced. "Is it weird to ask? I'm going to ask."

"It's less weird than assuming," Van said, and the joke steadied him just enough.

Jeremiah lifted a hand to Van's jaw and missed, then found it on the second try, fingers a little clumsy, palm warm. He leaned in and kissed him.

It wasn't cinematic. Their noses forgot math. Their teeth said hello by accident. Van made a noise he'd be embarrassed about later, and Jeremiah smiled against his mouth, and somehow that made them get it right. There—there it was. Soft. Braver than a whisper, smaller than a shout. The kind of kiss that felt like a window opening in a stuffy room.

When they pulled back, foreheads touched. Van didn't open his eyes immediately because he wanted to memorize the dark with Jeremiah this close in it.

"Okay," Jeremiah breathed, and it sounded like a decision. "Okay."

Van found a laugh. "We are disasters."

"We're excellent," Jeremiah corrected, and kissed him again, better—because practice does what practice does.

A shoe squeaked in the hall. They sprang apart like freshmen. Jeremiah grabbed a pencil from the stand and pretended to care deeply about a dotted half note. Van stared at the metronome like it was the most beautiful triangle he'd ever seen.

The hallway noise moved on.

Jeremiah set the pencil down. "We're careful," he said. "At church, especially. But I'm tired of pretending I don't want to sit next to you."

"At school," Van said, surprised by how easily the words came, "we can be... adjacent."

"Adjacent," Jeremiah repeated, smiling. "In geometry that means we share a side."

"We do," Van said, and felt his ears go hot.

They left separately, which is a kind of safety that still stings. At the vending machines, Tariq materialized like a plot twist and bought a Diet Coke with theatrical sighs.

"You two have 'music theory tutoring' faces," he announced, delighted. "I approve. Remember to hydrate. Love dries you out."

"Good afternoon, Tariq," Van said, trying to look like something other than a person whose mouth had just learned a new language.

Tariq leaned close to Van's ear. "You look happy."

Van didn't try to stop the smile. "I am," he said, and he didn't whisper it.

That night, they were brave in small ways. Jeremiah sat close enough at McDonald's that their knees argued under the table and lost. Dana clocked it immediately and smirked like a fairy godmother who was also a bouncer. Colby told a story about practice that got funnier only because he laughed at himself. Seth sang harmony with the fries. Tariq lifted a ketchup packet in a toast. "To the soft revolution," he declared. "May it always keep us."

Van walked into his house later with salt on his fingers and the taste of a practice room still in his mouth. His father sat in the recliner in full command position; his mother folded laundry like she could iron the day flat.

"How was choir?" Mr. Shelton asked, which meant *Who saw you sing so I can say I was there.*

"Good," Van said, which meant *Mine.* He went to his room, slid Mrs. Whitaker's marked-up score from his folder, copied one crooked measure into his notebook, and wrote in the margin: *we survived.*

Then he lay there smiling at the ceiling until sleep found him like a lake finds a stone.

"Not every invitation to the altar is an invitation from God."

— —AUNT SHEILA

CHAPTER 29
ALTARS AND EXITS

"Door's open," Youth Pastor Lane said when Van tapped the frame. His office smelled like Expo markers and bulk coffee. A print on the wall tried to talk him into Micah 6:8; a plastic ficus tried to remember how to be a tree.

"I'm trying to be honest with God," Van said, hands flat on his knees. "But every time I start, I hear twenty people in my head telling me what honesty is supposed to sound like."

Lane nodded the kind of nod that means *I'm listening.* "You can talk here," he said.

So Van did. About camp. About the nurse's pin and the way it had felt like a light. About the quiet with someone special that wasn't absence at all. Knowing this conversation was about Van figuring this out and not accidentally telling the Youth Pastor that his boss's son was his special person.

About the night in his grandmother's house when truth climbed out of his mouth and sat in his lap and didn't bite.

Lane's eyes were kind. They stayed kind even when he turned the conversation toward "design" and "purity" and "bearing a cross." He didn't sneer. He didn't weaponize. He just placed stones in a path he thought was safe and said, "Walk."

"How long?" Van asked, voice calm. "How long is the 'deny yourself' supposed to last?"

"All my life," Lane said softly, like he was telling the truth about himself too. "All of ours."

Van left with a heart that felt like it had sat too close to a fire. Warmed and raw. He told Lane thanks. He meant it. He also wanted to run until the wind stole the taste of the words.

Sunday night, the sanctuary had the under-attended feel of the second service at a church where the first one pays the light bill. Pastor Rich was at the couples' retreat with Denise, with Van's parents, with Uncle David and Aunt Leslie. Lane had the pulpit and a tie that made him look like he'd borrowed adulthood and was trying not to wrinkle it.

The youth filled three pews. Dana slid in and bumped Van's shoulder. "If he starts listing dangers of TikTok, I'm faking glossophobia and leaving," she muttered.

Avery shushed her theatrically and whispered, "Keep saying 'culture' and somebody's Sunday bulletin will grow a column.""

Lane's message started with lost sheep and drifted to modern snares and just when Van let himself exhale—okay, this would be general—Lane looked up from his notes and said, "Van?"

Van stood because that's what your body does when a microphone says your name.

"Come up, son," Lane said, voice soft. "I asked him earlier if I could ask this of him." (He hadn't. Van saw regret flick through Lane's eyes like a fish in shallow water.) "This young man wants strength. He wants purity. He wants to honor Christ more than culture. We're going to pray for him."

A hum passed through the room. Agreement. Relief. Some dear, earnest people stood because this was what love looked like to them: hands, blessings, a tide of prayer rising over a bowed head.

Van felt the first palm graze his shoulder and his lungs misfire. High ceiling. Loud lights. The carpet's red screamed. He looked up and found Jeremiah, three pews back, gripping the wood with both hands like he could hold the building up by himself. Jeremiah shook his head once. A small *no. Not this way. I'm here.*

Van stepped backward. A hand followed. Someone murmured, "It's okay, honey," in a voice that meant *I wish this were easier for you too.*

"No," Van said. Not loud. Clear. He turned. He walked. The aisle stretched. He didn't run. He moved like he wanted to run and believed in dignity anyway.

The lobby breathed him out into the night. The air hit his face cold and saved him and punched him at the same time. His chest stuttered. Panic arrived the way storms do in summer— fast, full, unapologetic. He bent over the hood of a car and pressed his palms to his sternum like a man keeping a door shut in the wind.

A hand landed at the back of his neck, warm and human. "Look at me," Jeremiah said, forehead close enough to feel like shelter. "Borrow my breath. In with me. Out with me."

They did. In. Out. The first felt like drowning slower. The second felt like finding the shallow shelf in a lake with your toes. By the fourth, the sky had edges again.

The doors whispered open and shut behind them. A few people peeked out and then had the good sense to look away. Dana came and planted herself five feet out like a bouncer at a holy nightclub. "Back it up, saints," she said, gentle and sharp. "Space is part of grace."

Tariq fanned Van with a bulletin like a benevolent aunt. "He's fine," he told no one and everyone. "He's breathing.

Which is what you should all be doing. In through the nose," he demonstrated, "out through the parts of you that gossip."

Lane stood in the doorway, hands lifted halfway to helpless. His face looked like the moment a good man realizes his timing was bad. He didn't come closer. He tipped his chin in apology Van would accept later, and slipped back inside.

Van's hands stopped shaking first. Then his knees. Then his mouth could form a smile that didn't hurt.

"You okay?" Jeremiah asked, voice barely above the crickets.

"No," Van said, honest. "But I'm not drowning."

"Okay," Jeremiah said, and his thumb traced a quick crescent at the base of Van's skull, then fell away. "That's enough for right now."

From inside, the youth sang a closing chorus, thin and earnest. Outside, under the lamplight's flicker, two boys learned how to breathe like choir kids who'd found the right pitch.

Dana exhaled, shoulders dropping. "We're getting fries," she declared, the way queens make law.

Tariq bowed. "And a milkshake for our hero."

Jeremiah looked at Van, a question without a question mark. Van nodded. "Yeah," he said, voice still small, finally his. "Let's go."

They walked to the cars together, close enough to feel like one body moving through weather. Van didn't look back at the church. Not tonight.

CHAPTER 30
ASH WEDNESDAY ON A MONDAY

Monday felt like someone had wrung the color out of the halls and left everything hanging to dry. Word traveled the way it always did in a small school—through lockers and homerooms and the back row of Algebra. "They had him up front" turned into "They made him repent" turned into "He ran from the altar." Each telling sanded off what it didn't understand.

Dana let the rumor skim off her like rain on new wax. "If anybody wants to lay hands on me," she said at lunch, voice bright as silverware, "they can help me carry this tray." She slid into the seat across from Van and planted her elbows. "How's the air in your lungs?"

"Occupied, but civil," Van said.

Avery tipped his carton of milk in a toast. "To oxygen and discretion. Preferably in that order."

Across the cafeteria, Colby and Seth lobbed grapes at each other, then pretended it was a drill for some imaginary sport that combined football and duck-and-cover. Jeremiah threaded through the tables with that soft step he had, a shy hello tucked into the lift of his chin. He didn't sit right next to Van. He sat close enough to be the next note.

"Lane cornered me after school," Dana said. "Apologized. Said his mouth ran faster than his discernment. I told him mine does too, and it's why I keep gum."

"He wants to see me," Van murmured. "One-on-one. Not a trap. A real sorry."

"Take the sorry," Avery said, peeling an orange with surgical focus. "And if he hands you a purity pamphlet, fold it into a paper crane and set it free."

After last bell, Van found the youth room quiet as a book left open. Lane sat with his tie loosed and a coffee gone cold.

"I hurt you," Lane said, before Van could manufacture anything polite.

"You scared me," Van answered, not unkind.

Lane nodded, slow. "I thought I was inviting strength. I made a spectacle."

They let the words sit between them like two boys who'd both gotten lost and found the same ditch.

"I don't know what to say that doesn't sound like a fix," Lane added. "You don't need fixing. You need... space."

"I need time," Van said. "And a God who wasn't embarrassed to stand near me outside."

Lane rubbed his eyes. "He wasn't," he said. "I wasn't either. I'm sorry I made it look like we were."

On his way out, Van passed the church bulletin board. Someone had taped up a flyer for the Watch Night service—sing-in-the-new-year in block letters—and beneath it, a sign-up sheet for cookies. Aunt Leslie's name had already claimed three lines.

At Magnolia that evening, the grill hissed like an old argument settling. Marlene slid a slice of chocolate pie onto a plate and pushed it across to Van with a fork made of kindness. "I don't have words," she said. "So I have pie."

Frank flipped a burger and said to the air, "Prayers are only good as the hands that deliver 'em."

By the time the dinner rush softened, the bell on the door gave a ceremonial jingle. Mr. Shelton came in with two church men trailing. He took a booth by the window and waited just long enough to make it awkward before waving Van over with a look-at-us grin.

"This boy," he announced to the table, "is learning to stand tall in a crooked world."

Van poured water without spilling. "Sweet tea?" he asked the deacon.

"Half and half," the man said, wincing like sugar was sin.

Mr. Shelton leaned back, palms tented. "I was at a retreat," he began, launching into a story that had more laughter than content. When it bent toward a lesson, he glanced up to see if anyone was admiring his bend.

He left without tipping well. Frank watched through the pass and made a small sound in his throat.

"Family discount," he deadpanned.

"Family surcharge," Marlene corrected, sliding Van a to-go cup of coffee for the ride home. "The kind that keeps your hands warm even when your house is full of cold."

CHAPTER 31

TAG SALE

They called it an estate sale in the paper, but the cardboard signs on the corner just said SALE in thick black marker. Strangers came in polite waves—women with lists, men with tape measures that snapped like tongues, a boy dragging a mother toward a box of marbles.

Van worked the breakfast shift and came late, apron still in his pocket. By the time he turned down her street, the good parking was gone. The yard looked like memory thrown to the wind and tied back with price tags.

Leslie held court at the card table like a fair banker. "Cash only," she sang, her pen tapping the tally sheet. "No, ma'am, that quilt is already on hold. Yes, sir, the ladder-back chairs are firm."

Uncle David walked the rooms with a clipboard, a sheriff in his own mind. Two aunts hovered near the jewelry like bees in their Sunday best.

Emmalee found Van on the porch steps, cheeks warm, hands empty. "They wanted twenty dollars for her recipe box," she said, outraged on principle. "I told the lady it wasn't food you could buy."

.R. GRAY-HEIM

"What did she say?"

"She said she was early," Em sniffed. "Like that was a character trait."

They went inside together because some tours you don't do alone. The living room's bones showed. On the end table where the emerald lamp used to sit, a circle of faded varnish glowed like a halo left behind. A man in a seed cap tried to negotiate down the price of the clock that had ticked their naps into shape. Van had to put his hands in his pockets to keep from lifting the clock and running.

In the bedroom, a stranger admired the bedspread with a polite sadness people keep in the trunk for funerals and yard sales. "Hand-stitched," she said to no one, "such small stitches." She didn't buy it.

Van found small things because small things looked back and recognized him. The Tupperware measuring cup with the handle cracked but faithful. A deck of cards with four queens gone soft at the corners from being favorites. The thimble with a dent where a careless twelve-year-old had stepped on it and Grandma had laughed and made him mashed potatoes anyway. He set them aside near the cash box, and Leslie wrote them down without looking at him.

"How much for grief?" he asked, too low for anyone but Em to hear.

"Costs everything," she said. "We get it wholesale."

On his way out, a woman stopped him, palm on his sleeve. "Your grandmother taught my Sunday school class one winter," she said. "She used to bring ginger cookies with sugar that crunched loud and said, 'God doesn't mind if you make a joyful noise with your teeth.'"

Van laughed and felt something unclench. "That sounds like her."

"Take the cookie jar," the woman added, nodding toward the kitchen. "I don't need it. You do."

In the kitchen, the jar waited—white ceramic, blue windmill, a chip on the rim big enough to be a personality trait. He lifted it and knew he'd carry it like an inheritance.

Back at the card table, Van placed his small pile. Leslie totaled quickly, wrote a number as tidy as her hair. Van paid with tips wadded into a neat stack and cleared his throat.

"You could've called me," he said, not angry now, just tired.

"We needed to keep momentum," Leslie repeated, as if they were still talking about weather.

Shelia emerged from the hallway like a storm that had chosen not to break. "Momentum is what a family uses to roll over quiet boys," she murmured. "Don't worry. I bit ankles where needed."

On the porch, Van and Em sat with the jar between them like a third sibling. Cars came and went. The clock went, finally, to a woman who cried when she lifted it and said, "This will keep time at my house." Van let her.

That night, the living room at home looked more like a museum exhibit titled OUR FAMILY, curated by someone who'd read the pamphlet. The emerald lamp threw its patient green. The afghan lay obedient. Van set the cookie jar on the counter and didn't say what he wanted to say.

Mr. Shelton came in from the garage and gave the jar a noncommittal glance. "Hope you didn't overpay," he said.

Van exhaled through his nose. "I paid exactly what it costs," he said, and went to his room before his words grew teeth.

CHAPTER 32

WATCH NIGHT, BONFIRE

December slid toward the edge of itself and pretended not to notice. The church put out a sign for Watch Night, the letters slotted in crooked, as if even the plastic wasn't convinced. Avery's aunt announced a bonfire at her place—end of the cut-through road, the one with the sycamore that looked like it had a story to tell.

"Decision time," Dana said, hands on hips in the choir room, the day before. "Hymns till midnight or smoke in our hair and somebody's uncle playing guitar out of tune."

Jeremiah drummed his fingers on his binder. "Dad expects me at church." He kept his tone neutral, the way a man turns down a radio without admitting it was too loud.

"Mom expects all of us there," Van said, and tasted the shape of that truth. "But I don't know if I can sing my way into another year without breathing first."

Avery fanned himself with his folder. "Reader, they went to the fire," he narrated, eyes glinting.

They went.

The night sprawled friendly and imperfect. The bonfire hurled sparks at the sky and made up constellations the way drunk men make up advice. Someone brought a pot of chili and too few spoons. Seth tried to cook a hot dog and set it ablaze like an offering. Colby showed up late, helmet hair under a beanie, grin jammed crooked.

"Coach would die if he knew I wasn't watching the ball drop with Jesus," he said, then added, "Don't tell my dad I said that."

A guitar passed from hand to hand and landed, inevitably, with a boy who knew three chords and believed all songs could be negotiated into them. They sang anyway. "Wagon Wheel" fought with "I'll Fly Away" and nobody lost. Laughter layered the cold until the cold gave up.

Jeremiah stood on the far side of the fire, face flickering between light and shadow, eyes on Van like a compass. Midnight came the way midnight always does—sudden and entirely predictable. Somebody yelled "ten!" too early, and somebody else corrected them, and everybody counted together because it's easier to believe in time when you do it in a group.

At zero, the sky above the cut-through road bloomed with cheap fireworks from a nearby yard—white chrysanthemums, red stars that sputtered like the end of a hymn. Cheering rose without a leader.

Jeremiah moved, slow and sure, around the edge of the flames until he was beside Van. Not touching. Touching in a different language.

"Hi," he said, a smile tucked into the word.

"Hi," Van said, mouth unsteady.

"Can I—" Jeremiah began, then didn't finish, then did. "I want to kiss you while the year is new."

They stepped into the dark just beyond the blast radius of smoke. The fire's breath warmed their backs; the night's cold woke their faces. Jeremiah lifted a hand and cupped Van's jaw like a fragile thing you learn isn't fragile. The kiss made no sound. It didn't need to. It was clumsy in the way first dances are—two people learning where the other keeps his center—and it was beautiful because it decided to be.

When they parted, someone on the other side of the fire whooped for a reason that belonged to them. Van laughed against Jeremiah's shoulder, the sound surprised out of him.

"Happy new year," Jeremiah whispered.

"Happy," Van said, and meant it in a way he hadn't meant anything out loud in a long time.

On the drive home, smoke rode their jackets into the car and refused to leave. Dana rolled down her window and sang something off-key on purpose. Avery dozed in the back seat like a glamorous cat and woke only to say, "We did not combust. I call that a win."

Van pulled into the driveway at exactly the same minute the church parking lot across town let out its sleepy parade. He sat in the car a beat longer, forehead on the wheel, letting the cold come in and settle the heat behind his eyes.

In bed, he said the small prayer he'd been saying since June —keep us—and slept before the old clock on his dresser could tick twice.

CHAPTER 33

TABLE SEVEN

They came in with luggage still in the trunk and retreat glow in their faces. Dana saw them from the hostess stand and palmed the seating chart like a poker player on a good run.

"Table Seven," she told Van under her breath, then louder for their benefit: "Right this way, Mr. and Mrs. Shelton—best table in the house."

Marlene arched an eyebrow. "Best because the light's flattering," she murmured. "And because our waiter knows when to keep the coffee full and the commentary empty."

Van wiped his palms on his apron and carried water like it was china. His mother's eyes skimmed him with a look that tried to be normal and landed on proud. His father sat with a stretch that said Here I am.

"Well!" Mr. Shelton boomed, before anyone asked. "You'll never guess what the speaker said about husbands and leadership." He didn't wait for a guess.

"Specials are on the board," Van said. "Meatloaf's good tonight."

Mrs. Shelton folded her napkin with too much attention.

"We surprise you," she said, softer than her smile. "Your daddy was craving coffee that didn't taste like fellowship hall."

Dana refilled a tea like a guardian angel. As she slid by Van, she hissed, "They don't know. Luggage still in the car. You're safe for thirty minutes."

Van breathed. "Thank you."

"Also they tipped well last time they were here," she added. "Let's aim for consistency."

Between courses, Mr. Shelton held court with the couple in the next booth—the one where the husband wore his tie like a concession and the wife laughed at the right times. "My boy," he said to them, with a proud thumb thrown Van's way, "is learning discipline. Work, school, church. It's what makes a man."

"Men also tip," Marlene said, materializing with pie slices, smile sweet as icing and sharp as a blade. "And mothers listen." She set a piece of chess pie in front of Mrs. Shelton with a wink so quick only a woman would catch it.

The bill came in a black vinyl folder, the kind that always felt like it contained secrets. Mr. Shelton tucked bills with a flourish, lifted the pen, signed his name big enough to be read from space.

When Van slid the folder back, he didn't leave yet. He stood there with the practiced half-smile of a boy who has served and is deciding whether to speak.

"Can I—" he started, then steadied. "When I get home, could we talk?"

His mother looked up first. "Of course," she said. "We'll be up."

His father tilted his head. "About what?" The tone that implies he'd prefer the short version right here.

"About me," Van said. "About... what comes next."

Mr. Shelton opened his mouth—some combination of joke and sermon jockeying for exit.

Mrs. Shelton touched his sleeve. "We'll be up," she repeated, stealing the scene back with a quiet hand.

Back in the kitchen, Dana caught Van by both shoulders and shook him the way you steady a picture frame. "You don't owe them a thesis," she said. "You owe them your truth."

Avery appeared with a coffee stirrer like a wand. "And if the truth gets stuck in your throat, I have six monologues about identity I can lend you for the low price of a hug."

"I'll start with my own," Van said, a smile lifting despite the lead in his limbs.

"You'll start with breath," Marlene called, topping off a cup. "Then words. In that order."

He drove home slow, the kind of slow that looks like caution and is actually courage. At red lights, he practiced, mouth moving, hands loose on the wheel. The same two sentences, over and over, until they felt like they belonged to his voice.

Grandma, he said silently at one stop, look at me. He pictured her at the stove, humming off-key. I'm bringing it to the table you set.

The house glowed, familiar and staged. He parked under the maple and let the engine tick itself quiet.

"There's a difference between rehearsing courage and using it; both are holy."

———VAN'S JOURNAL

CHAPTER 34

THE DRIVEWAY REHEARSAL

He cut the headlights and the driveway became a place with a secret all its own. The porch light had that moth-spangled halo it always wore. Somewhere down the block, a dog barked like nobody had explained the calendar to him and he was sounding the alarm just in case.

Van leaned forward, folded his arms on the steering wheel, and put his forehead down on them like an altar.

"All right," he said. "We're going to do this like choir— breathe on four, enter on one, mean it."

He said it out loud because words in the air behaved better than words in his skull. "Mom. Dad. I love you." Good start. True. "I need to tell you something that's been true longer than I've known how to say it." His mouth shook. His hands didn't.

He tried on a joke and took it off. He tried on a sermon and threw it in the back seat where it belonged. He kept the simple thing.

"I'm gay," he said into the safe darkness. "I didn't choose it. I didn't catch it. It's not a test I'm failing. It's me. I'm still your son. I am also... me."

He waited for the car to answer, which is not a thing cars do. Instead, the maple shifted and let go of one brown leaf that traveled the windshield like a small blessing.

"Grandma," he added, out of habit and hope, "if you've got your ear to the floor, I'm stepping in. Hum something. Anything."

In his mind, she hummed the line she'd always half-forgotten and half-sung louder to make up for it: here I raise mine Ebenezer. He smiled without meaning to. He reached over to the passenger seat and picked up the green hymnbook he'd tucked there for luck. He tapped its spine with two fingers.

"Okay," he told the book, the house, God, himself. "Go."

He opened the car door and the cold took his breath like it wanted to be in charge and then handed it back. The key felt old in his palm, which steadied him. He stepped up onto the porch. The boards said hello in their winter voices.

He opened the door.

Inside, the television kept up a brave mutter. His mother was curled on the couch under the green afghan, hair loose for once, hands wrapped around a mug like a small animal. His father sat in the recliner with his slippers on, eyes on the screen and on whatever script he preferred for comfort.

Van stepped in and the room tipped its gaze toward him as if he were a guest and the owner of the house at the same time.

"You made good time," his father said. "Your mother said you wanted to—"

"Talk," Van finished, and heard the word land.

He closed the door behind him and turned the lock because some conversations prefer privacy even when they don't need security. He took one breath the way Mrs. Whitaker had drilled it into him—low, open, patient.

His mother set down her mug. "We're listening," she said, voice steadying itself. The green afghan slid a little and caught on her knees the way old things do when they're trying their best.

Van looked from her to his father and back again. He felt the shape of the words in his mouth like a key finally finding the right teeth.

He opened his mouth.

—

End of Book Two.

Epilogue — Jeremiah, Keeping Watch

The parsonage kept quiet like a church after benediction. The radiator ticked. Somewhere in the living room, his father's sermon notes rustled as sleep rearranged them. Denise had left a retreat brochure folded on the kitchen table, a coffee ring making a halo on "Renewal."

Jeremiah sat on the edge of his bed with his boots still on. The window gave him the black lace of the pecan tree and a slice of sky thin as a ribbon. Cold pressed the pane. He pressed back.

He didn't have a clock that mattered, but his ribs kept time. When they did that particular slow drum—four in, four out— he stood, shrugged into his jacket, and eased down the back steps to the stoop.

Breath showed itself in the air, small white testimonies. The church steeple lifted a shoulder against the dark. Across town, lights burned in ordinary squares. He didn't know which one was the right square, but he knew what hour it was in a house that wasn't his: the hour a boy would come in from the cold and stand in a doorway and ask two people to look at him all the way.

"Keep him," Jeremiah said into his scarf. He didn't ask for outcomes. Just for breath and room. "Keep his voice from shaking more than it needs to. Keep the truth from sounding like an apology."

He remembered the way Van had practiced in parking lots —how words moved better when the world was bigger than the room that would hold them. He matched his breathing to that memory, the way you match pitch in a hymn you didn't think you knew.

A dog barked, then didn't. A car turned at the corner and didn't stop. He stayed anyway, hands in his pockets, counting to sixty and starting over, like faith with a metronome.

"Grandma Sheldon," he added, not sure if you could borrow someone else's heaven and doing it anyway, "if you're listening where he is, hum something steady."

He didn't hear the door across town open. He believed it did. He kept his place on the stoop like a marker in a song, the kind you don't sing out loud but hold, so the next note knows where to land. When the hour was over—however it ended— he would not ask for a report. He would just meet Van where the light found them next and breathe with him, four in, four out, until the year learned the tune.

About the Author

JR Gray-Heim is a North Carolina–based author whose work blends vivid storytelling with raw emotional depth, creating narratives that linger long after the last page. With a background as both a creative visionary and community builder, Gray-Heim writes with a voice that is as intimate as it is universal—capturing the weight of burden, resilience, and redemption in the human spirit.

Beyond writing, Gray-Heim is a salon owner, educator, and philanthropist, dedicated to elevating both art and community. When not immersed in his latest manuscript, he can be found designing intentional spaces, mentoring young artists, or championing local causes.

The Unburdened Series marks Gray-Heim's debut into the literary world—an exploration of the ties that bind us, the secrets that haunt us, and the strength it takes to break free.

ACKNOWLEDGMENTS

To my husband, **Adam** — your love, patience, and unwavering belief in me carried this story when I questioned whether I could. You have been my calm, my compass, and my constant reminder that authenticity is always worth the risk. This book exists because you never stopped believing in what I had to say. And to our son, **Caleb** — your courage, humor, and kindness have shown me what true strength looks like. Watching you grow into yourself has been one of my life's greatest honors.

You remind me daily why stories like this matter — because somewhere, someone is still trying to find their way home, too.

To my mentors, teachers, and creative guides — thank you for showing me how to shape chaos into story and emotion into truth. Your insight gave this book structure; your encouragement gave it courage.

To the early readers who saw the heart of *Burdens Beneath the Hymns* long before when it started as *Repentance of the Southern Burden* — your faith in these pages kept me going. You recognized the pulse of this story and pushed me forward when I couldn't see how to take another step.

And finally, to everyone who has ever carried the weight of their own story — this book is for you. The struggles we survive, the love we find, and the truths we learn to speak are not small things. You reminded me that healing doesn't come from perfection, but from being seen.

Thank you — truly — for allowing this story to find you.

— JR Gray-Heim